A *Merry* MURDEROUS MIDWINTER

DAHLIA DONOVAN

HOT TREE PUBLISHING

For information, contact the publisher, Tangled Tree Publishing.

WWW.HOTTREEPUBLISHING.COM

EDITING: HOT TREE EDITING

COVER DESIGNER: BOOKSMITH DESIGN

MAP DESIGN: THE ILLUSTRATED PAGE BOOK DESIGN

E-BOOK ISBN: 978-1-923252-25-7

PAPERBACK ISBN: 978-1-923252-26-4

ALSO BY DAHLIA DONOVAN

THE SKELETON CREW PARANORMAL COZY SERIES

A CURSE FOR SAMHAIN | A FATAL AUTUMNAL STEW | A MERRY MURDEROUS MIDWINTER

THE GRASMERE COTTAGE MYSTERY TRILOGY

DEAD IN THE GARDEN | DEAD IN THE POND | DEAD IN THE SHOP

MOTTS COLD CASE MYSTERY SERIES

POISONED PRIMROSE | PIERCED PEONY | PICKLED PETUNIA | PURLOINED POINSETTIA

LONDON PODCAST MYSTERY SERIES

COSPLAY KILLER | GHOST LIGHT KILLER | CROWN COURT KILLER

HONEY BEAR COSY MYSTERIES

HONEY MEAD MURDER | HONEY BEE MURDER | HONEY MOON MURDER

STAND-ALONE ROMANCES

AFTER THE SCRUM | AT WAR WITH A BROKEN HEART | FORGED IN FLOOD | FOUND YOU | ONE LAST HEIST | PURE DUMB LUCK | HERE COMES THE SON | ALL LATHERED UP | NOT EVEN A MOUSE | FARM TO

A MERRY MURDEROUS MIDWINTER

THE SKELETON CREW PARANORMAL COZY SERIES
BOOK 3

DAHLIA DONOVAN

HOT TREE PUBLISHING

To my found family

SOUTH MYRDDIN

1

HYDE

"Well? How goes the installation?" Hyde joined their two cats at the end of the bookshop counter. Mortar lounged gracefully in all her silvery Persian splendour, with her blue eyes taking in everything. They gently ran their hands along her fur. "That's exciting, isn't it?"

Pestle, on the other hand, seemed five seconds away from managing some sort of chaos. He was their fluffy ginger menace of a cat with his bright yellow eyes and long orange-marmalade fur. They often wondered if someone had shrunk a lion down at some point to create him — something not quite out of the question given the myriad of magical folk and creatures in the village.

Hyde Snodgrass had been the owner of Between

the Leaves for decades. It was the lone bookshop in South Myrddin, a tiny, picturesque village on Loch Bard in the Scottish Highlands. They'd lived there since coming as a young vampire close to a century ago.

South Myrddin was home to many an abandoned child. Magical foundlings of every variety made the village what it was. According to local lore, Myrddin had founded it for that very purpose.

"Careful. Don't knock my signs over." Hyde righted the Hello sign. It helped villagers know when they were okay to chat. The other side said Shh, for quiet days. They shifted Pestle further down the counter. "Behave yourself."

The other sign was flipped to They. It had been decidedly a "they" sort of day when Hyde had woken up. The opposite side said Her. One of the local witches, Florence Batch, had come up with the idea ages ago.

She had been one of the coven leaders. She'd been murdered back in October. Hyde still struggled with the idea that the vibrant crone was gone.

Shaking the melancholy away, Hyde inched closer to where Aadil Fadel was installing glorious new stained-glass windows. The djinn and glazier had already put in the new shop door, which had equally beautiful and colourful panels inserted within the solid oak. He did amazing work and was incredibly fast.

It had only been a few weeks back when the father of Amalia Bassani, a local succubus and restaurateur, had attempted to burn down the shop after murdering his own son. That had failed. The door and windows had been damaged when Hyde had launched him through it. In their defence, he'd been attempting to kill them.

Aadil had promised to fix up the beloved windows and make them even better. He'd gone above and beyond. It was three panels showing a stunning autumnal view of the village and loch. They had no idea how he'd done it so quickly. The two stained-glass sections in the door showed Mortar and Pestle in all their glorious splendour.

Hyde waved at Aadil, catching his attention. They waited until he had a clear view of their hands and mouth before speaking to him. He had a better handle on lip-reading than they did on BSL, or British Sign Language. "Would you like some tea and biscuits? Or I can run down to Roasted and Toasted for coffee and a pastry?"

Aadil shook his head, signing no. "I'm almost

finished. I've got another job this afternoon about thirty minutes away, so I can't hang around."

Hyde appreciated him signing slowly. It gave them more time to understand what he'd said. "Fair enough. You're an angel, Aadil. Thank you."

"Not an angel. A djinn." He winked; his dark brown eyes always glinted with a hint of mischief. He brushed the dust out of his black hair and beard before raising his hands again. "Any new scrolls for me?"

Hyde spun around to check the shop computer before turning back. "Not yet. I've a lead on another Egyptian one, but it might be one I find on my summer adventure."

"Just let me know." He tapped his knuckles against the last window. "Putting this one in now. Then I'll be done."

Many of the villagers came to the shop to find rare books, scrolls, or anything paper-related. Hyde often strayed far from South Myrddin in the summers, hunting for new treasures to bring home. Aadil, when he wasn't making beautiful creations out of glass, loved finding obscure texts from his first home. He'd never shared how long ago he'd left Egypt.

It was tricky with djinns, who always appeared far younger than they looked. But Hyde couldn't say anything; they hadn't technically aged since their thirties. Nor had many of the other villagers. It all depended on what flavour of magical being one was.

They'd been the same chubby, ginger, autistic vampire for close to a century. There were so many myths about vampires. Garlic, for example, was delicious and didn't bother them at all.

Mirrors? Hyde could see themselves perfectly fine —they just didn't need to. They knew what they'd see if they looked into one.

Short, curly red hair was usually hidden by a hat of some variety. Today, it was a pale grey beanie that Teresa, their girlfriend, had knitted for them. Bright blue eyes contrasted against their incredibly pale skin.

Teresa Vega lived in the converted double-decker bus parked outside the bookshop. She was far cooler than Hyde could ever dream of being with her piercing, tattoos, sleek brown hair, and soulful voice. Hyde had been lost from the moment the witch had strolled into their life.

Someone had once told them they had a cheeky, cherub face. Hyde had hissed at them. Tiny fangs hadn't been overly threatening. It had taken a while to grow into them.

Hyde had all the air of a dapper young lad from

the 1920s, particularly today with their knitted jumper and the collared shirt underneath. Their tweed trousers had the perfect length, tailored because finding the right fit when they were barely five foot four was nigh impossible. *I need another pair of these.*

"Stop admiring your trousers." Bram squeezed past Aadil into the bookshop.

"Ah. Our semiferal wandering bard." Hyde frowned when he hopped up to sit on the counter. "Bram."

"Just saying hello to the cats." Bram had returned to the village a month back after a lengthy absence. One of the oldest fae in Scotland, probably the world, he'd been away dealing with the Seelie Court. He'd tamed his wild brown hair into a loose bun. His guitar was, as always, strapped to his back. It only seemed to highlight his lithe yet muscular form. "How is the morning treating you, *mo chridhe*?"

"I am not your heart. Stop it. Makes me feel like I'm this massive beating heart just flopping around on the pavement." Hyde knew he wouldn't stop. He took it as a personal mission to be as disruptive as possible. "What chaos are we causing this morning?"

"Me? Chaos?"

"It's in your veins. What have you done? You're

never usually this chipper so early in the morning." Hyde typically saw Bram dragging himself from his lighthouse on the edge of the village no earlier than noon. "Well?"

"I have a rock garden."

Hyde blinked several times. They glanced over at Mortar, who yawned before returning to Bram. "A rock garden?"

"Aye. In front of the lighthouse. I've arranged them along the windowsill."

"Bram." Hyde spoke very slowly. "Bram. Why have you arranged pebbles along a windowsill in the lighthouse?"

"Outside the lighthouse. How else will they get sunlight?" Bram smiled brightly when they rubbed their eyes tiredly. "You've missed me, haven't you?"

"Do the pebbles need sunlight?"

"Arthur gets quite grumpy without it," Bram said with a straight face, as if he hadn't named a random rock and claimed the thing needed sunlight to thrive. "Cernunnos prefers the south-facing windows."

"This might be a silly question."

"No such thing." He waved off their concern.

"A complete lie. I've known you long enough to know there are definitely silly questions. Ones you usually ask." Hyde soldiered on, trying to make sense out of the fae's nonsense. "Have you named one of your rocks after the Celtic horned god?"

"He named himself. As did King Arthur."

"First, Arthur was mythical. Probably." Hyde had read loads of contradictory material on Camelot, the Round Table, and even Merlin. They'd been drawn to the legends because of living in South Myrddin. "Second, and far more importantly, how exactly did he name himself?"

"The rocks are possessed."

Hyde bitterly regretted running out of blood wine. They did have a bottle of non-alcoholic blood in the fridge upstairs in their flat above the shop, but it wasn't the same. As a vampire, they consumed both liquid and regular food. "Your rock garden, which isn't a garden, is filled with possessed rocks."

"Correct."

Hyde eyed his mischievous smirk with suspicion. "You're doing this to annoy Emrys, aren't you? Why else would you pick King Arthur and a Celtic god important to druids?"

Bram didn't answer, and with a laboured sigh, Hyde turned their attention away from the silliness of faes to focus on their work. They had received a new shipment of books early in the morning. It was time to find new homes on one of the many shelves in the shop.

All of the shelves littered around the room were solid oak. Most had been handmade by Ada Senft, a local dryad, who helped run the orchard on the outskirts of the village and happened to be a skilled carpenter. The wood worked with Ada, creating unique pieces that seemed sculpted for the bookshop.

Strings of faint burgundy lights made by Morrigan, the postmistress and witch, ran along the tops of the shelves. They twinkled merrily, casting an autumnal hue around the room all year round. Hyde adored them.

Morrigan had run the village post office since Hyde could remember. She worked with her seeing-eye crow perched on her shoulder most days. Odin was a clever bird who tended to be very protective of his human. Both usually came to the knitting circle, lovingly called the Skeleton Crew, who met in the bookshop at least once a week.

The knitting group took up one corner of the shop near the fireplace. There was a mixture of armchairs, and everyone in the group had a favourite. They gathered mostly to gossip; crafting was just the excuse.

"How did your beautiful stained glass break?"

Bram interrupted their thoughts as they opened the first box.

"I launched a demon through it. You've heard the story about ten times now, Bram." Hyde didn't even bother glancing up at him.

"I'm aware. It amuses me every time I imagine you kicking Enzo Bassani arse-first through the glass."

"To be fair, I'm not entirely sure which part of him went through first." Hyde set a stack of werewolf-vampire romance novels on the counter. They'd promised to save one for Emrys. "I was too busy making sure he didn't hurt one of my cats."

"Allow me the beautiful vision." Bram draped himself dramatically along the counter until Pestle threatened him with one sharp claw. "Back, foul beast. I surrender."

"You're lounging in his sunspot." Hyde carried the stack of books over to the shelf reserved for newer releases in the romance section. They carefully placed them in the right spot and then wandered over to one of the locked cases. "Do you want the Nessie folklore anthology, or am I keeping this one?"

"Ah, poor Ness MacDougal. No one knows where she went. All they know is flowers appear where her beloved warlock was murdered. Every year. The same bouquet." Bram lowered his voice, adding a melodic lilt to the words. "Ah, wee Nessie's bitter regret."

"Not the title of the book."

"Maybe you should write it." Bram winked at them. "Ah, I sense an Emrys disturbance in the air. Have a good morning, wee fanged one. Keep the Nessie folklore. Maybe it'll inspire you."

"Honestly," Hyde sighed. "It's too early in the morning for you to be... you."

2

TERESA

WAKING UP TO THE DARK WAS PART AND parcel of life in the Scottish Highlands in the winter. Teresa always had an early start. She'd done her morning rituals already, spending time at her altar. A little blessing in the hopes of a calm December and midwinter celebration. October and November had been troubling in parts with murder investigations.

Yule should be a time of celebration and reflection without the side of death.

Teresa drew her long brown hair into a ponytail. She wanted it out of her face while she prepped to open up Guac-A-Mole. *The mole won't make itself. I may be a witch, but I can't bibbity bobbity boo and have tacos.*

Her taco truck, technically taco bus, filled the lower half of a blue-and-cream vintage double-decker bus. The top floor had been renovated into a living space. A bit cramped, but she loved her little home.

She'd never regretted the move from Ireland to South Myrddin. Her mother had passed away, and her father almost immediately disappeared to his family home in Mexico. It had left her to find her own way in life. And that had led her to the welcoming embrace of the little village by the loch—and eventually Hyde.

Life had changed so much for her in the years since. She was part of the witch coven in the village and sang at least once a week at The Spiked Cauldron, the local pub. Falling in love with Hyde had definitely been the greatest part of her move.

Peering through the front windows when music caught her attention, Teresa spotted Emrys in front of the bookshop. He seemed to be starting some form of ritual, probably to adjust the wards because of the new windows and door. As the eldest druid, he took safety in the village seriously. No one ever quite knew exactly how old he was.

To her amusement, Bram was out there as well with his guitar out. He was strumming a jaunty tune and providing a lyrical running commentary on what Emrys was doing. The druid appeared to be doing his best to ignore the fae.

Teresa waved enthusiastically when she spotted Hyde in the shop doorway with one cat in their arms and the other draped across their shoulders. She grabbed her half-empty coffee mug and rushed over to her vampire. "Entertaining morning?"

"Bram has possessed rocks."

Teresa allowed the words to float around in her head, but they still didn't make sense. "I... don't know what to say to that."

"Cernunnos and King Arthur, apparently." Hyde spoke so mildly, as if they hadn't said two rocks were possessed by legendary figures.

"I'd think the Green Man had better things to do with his time." Teresa paused when Bram strolled closer to them. "Possessed rocks?"

"Want to meet them?" Bram smiled a little wildly.

"Not particularly." Teresa nodded to where Emrys continued to murmur in Gaelic. "Perhaps you shouldn't distract the man weaving ancient magic to protect our Hyde?"

Bram deflated visibly. "Fair enough. I shall stroll along my merry way and bring joy elsewhere."

Hyde leaned into Teresa when she wrapped an arm around their back, ignoring the glare from the cat on their shoulders. "His energy is loud. Like Pestle's yowling in the middle of the night when he wants a snack."

"A bit much this early in the morning?"

"Not quite early any longer, but I am all socialised out for the day." Hyde sighed tiredly. "Bottled blood isn't cutting it. I'm going to see if the bakery made the black pudding pastries this morning."

"How about I pop by The Golden Puff? Rosa had some spices delivered for me. You head in and switch your sign from Hello to Shh." Teresa suddenly remembered the packet that had arrived the day before. "Hang on. I have a present for you. An early Yule gift."

"Resa."

Ignoring Hyde's protest, Teresa darted back into her bus. She found the little cloth bag on the counter, grabbed it, and returned. It had been a custom item that had taken an annoyingly long time to arrive.

"Here."

Hyde shuffled Mortar over to Teresa and took the small cloth bag. They opened it cautiously, peering inside before breaking into a smile. "Resa. You didn't."

"Thought it was time you had something easy to travel." Teresa watched them lift out the four badges designed more like vintage tie pins. Each one had a different word created by a delicately inlaid gold wire over a black enamel background. It looked almost like an open book. "There's a Shh, Hello, They, and Her. This way, there's no reason for anyone to ever be confused."

Hyde held the badges up for Pestle to inspect where he sat on their shoulder. "They're beautiful."

"And designed with a bit of magic infused in the metal, so they shouldn't damage any of your lovely clothes." Teresa plucked up the Shh one and gently put it on Hyde's jumper. She took the They next and added it as well when they pointed to it. "There you go. All set."

Hyde had turned quite bashful, never sure what to do when a compliment was paid or kindness shown. They shoved the bag and other pins into their pocket, lunged forwards to kiss Teresa, grabbed Mortar from her arms, and fled into the shop. "Thank you."

Teresa exchanged a bemused grin with Emrys, who'd been quietly watching. "All finished with the protections?"

"Mostly updating the bell so it jingles more softly.

They'll hear it without being startled. Also added a secondary tone to identify anyone with ill intent." Emrys had always had a soft spot for Hyde. "You're good for our fanged foundling. Good," he said, turning and heading away from the shop.

The rest of the morning and afternoon flew by for Teresa. It was a cold but glorious December day. She closed up the taco truck before four; the sun had already begun to set.

They were definitely in for a cold winter, Teresa thought as she pulled a beanie over her head and grabbed her leather jacket. Tonight was going to be a fun pub night.

Until recently, The Spiked Cauldron had been run by the three eldest members of the village witch coven. With Florence's death, her partners in crime, Flossie Vandermark and Winifred Ferguson, continued the traditions of flowing ale and wild music. On most nights, Teresa joined several other musically gifted villagers to sing and dance their hearts away.

Stepping out of the bus, Teresa noted the lamps were already lit. The village streetlamps had been converted magically from old gas ones. No one quite knew how it had been done.

Local lore, as always, claimed Myrddin himself

had powered them. For centuries, they'd never once gone out. She often wished the history of the village had been written down and not passed orally from one foundling generation to the next.

Teresa wandered over to the bookshop, peering through the window to see Hyde had also changed. They'd spruced up a little, obviously intending to join her for a night at the pub. Mortar and Pestle sat on the counter, surveying their kingdom. She smiled when their vampire began heading towards the door. "Ready?"

"I am." Hyde pointed to the Hello badge on their collar. "Feeling more chatty."

"Did the quiet day in the bookshop help?" Teresa had done her best to dissuade people from heading in to speak with Hyde. Most had slipped notes through the door for the cats to collect. It was a system that worked on particular days when they felt sensitive to sound. "You had quite a stack of requests."

"I've got everyone's books ready for pick-up tomorrow." Hyde slipped their arm through Teresa's. "Thank you."

"Thank me by buying me a hot tea when my voice gets scratchy." Teresa leaned over to kiss them on the cheek. "Onwards to The Spiked Cauldron."

The pub slowly filled up as the evening went on.

Flossie and Winnie manned the bar. They'd brought out their usual midwinter decorations. Wreaths and garlands were strewn about. A simmer pot with oranges, cranberries, and other spices bubbled away over the fire. It filled the air with the scents of the season and hopes for the coming return of light.

Teresa smiled at the two older witches. They were glamorous and wild, always with a hint of mischief or a flash of temper. "Ready?"

"Go on then, lass," Flossie encouraged.

Teresa quieted everyone by moving to stand by Bram, who'd been strumming away on his guitar in a corner of the room. She hummed a few lines, smiling when he picked up the tune. Her gaze found Hyde in their secluded corner. They lifted their bottle of blood ale in salute. The words were on her lips in an instant. "The bright moon rose o'er a winter's night, its beauty dimmed by my lover's cold heart, it beats for me, though none can tell."

As Teresa continued to sing, her voice weaved its magic. Hyde's gaze settled on her chin. She knew every word of the ballad about a witch who'd fallen in love with a vampire held deeper meaning for the two of them.

One of the gifts from the Irish side of her family

had been a bardic one. There had been a long line of women who sang their magic into being. A lilting whisper that held the power to carry listeners away.

"Enough with the soppy shite," Queenie MacGavin called out when the last strains of the song died away. She laughed boisterously when the others jeered at her. "Give us a reel."

Rolling her eyes at the sheep shifter and village butcher, Teresa nodded to Bram. A few others picked up their instruments. A fiddle and a drum joined in as they played "Druid's Fair," one of the village's favourite reels.

The atmosphere was buoyant and joyful. Teresa allowed herself to be carried away by the melody. It was like riding a wave until Bram struck a different chord at the end of the last reel that jolted her back to shore.

Needing a break, Teresa squeezed through the crowd to the quiet corner where Hyde usually resided. They held out a mug of lemon honey tea with a hint of herb—a Winnie speciality. "Thank you."

Hyde shifted down to give Teresa room to join them. "You've been going a while."

"Good atmosphere. Everyone's shaking off the

heaviness from the past few months. A good start to the Yule season." Teresa clutched the mug in her hands, leaned closer, and placed her head on Hyde's shoulder. "It's always a little quieter over here."

"Flossie and Emrys worked together to muffle the sound. Not sure how they managed it." Hyde rested their head on Teresa's. "Maybe this is a good omen of things to come. Reels in The Spiked Cauldron weeks before the midwinter celebration."

"Here's hoping." Teresa kept an eye on where she could see Bram seated on the raised platform across the pub. He'd been casually strumming his guitar before suddenly taking a breath and beginning to sing. "Don't think I've heard that one."

"Hmm?" Hyde lifted their head and focused on Bram. "Balls."

"Hyde?"

"He's singing 'A Lonely Broken Druid.'"

"That sounds sad. What am I missing?" Teresa noticed Hyde searching the crowd. "Who are you looking for?"

"Emrys. The song is about him and supposedly a lost love. Neither he nor Bram has ever admitted who the man in question is." Hyde gave a deep sigh. "You can't deny that for all his chaos, his voice is beautiful."

Bram had a haunting tone to his singing. It made Teresa think of ancient forests with dark shadows and wild magic. She always carried people away with her music, but this was far different.

"I've always wondered if the Pied Piper was inspired by a fae. Not Bram. He'd have used a guitar, not any sort of flute." Hyde got to their feet and shook their head as if trying to rid themselves of the weight of his voice. "Can we go see if the Malt Moon is still open? I'm hungry."

Teresa finished her tea. She had no doubts the weight of the atmosphere had affected both of them. "I could do with some chips."

Of all the restaurants in the village, the Malt Moon usually stayed open the latest. Rees Mohan, one of the local werewolves, ran the fish and chips shop. He played guitar with Mortar and Pestle at least once a month, something Teresa found highly entertaining.

Ducking out of the pub, Teresa slipped her arm around Hyde. The two strolled slowly along Harbour Road. The pub and fish shop were on opposite ends of the lane, so they had a pleasant walk.

The scent of orange and cinnamon filled the air. There were several cauldrons bubbling away with the usual Yule mixtures. All a part of the magic of winter solstice in South Myrddin.

"It's going to be a good midwinter."

Hyde nodded a little hesitantly. "Let's hope October and November weren't omens of more dreadful things to come."

"Happy thoughts, Hyde. Happy thoughts."

3

HYDE

BEING IN BED WITH TERESA TOOK SOME getting used to. Hyde wasn't always ready to deal with conversation when their eyes opened. They carefully snuck out from under the covers, trying not to wake her.

Vampires didn't technically require sleep to survive, but Hyde had never met a nap they didn't enjoy. The cats certainly indulged in the art of rest as often as possible. Running a bookshop allowed them to have flexible hours, though a few nights a month, they stayed open late for the nocturnal few who wanted to browse once the sun had gone down.

After a quick shower, Hyde perused their wardrobe with just the flicker of candlelight. Their eyesight was good enough, and they really didn't need even that. They considered the array of autumnal-hued clothing. Some mornings, decisions were almost impossible.

"Balls," Hyde hissed. Executive dysfunction sometimes made their life incredibly hard, even supposedly easy tasks.

Mortar clambered over Pestle, stalking over to the edge of the bed. She waited patiently for Hyde to pick her up. The cat gestured insistently with her paw towards the open wardrobe.

"Going to help?" Hyde kept their voice low, not wanting to wake Teresa.

In no time at all, Mortar had selected three of Hyde's favourite comfort pieces of clothing. A burgundy turtleneck and dark forest-green trousers with a plaid waistcoat of a similar shade. They could easily throw on a cape or coat over it all.

The turtleneck wasn't always Hyde's go-to. Sometimes, it made them feel like they were being choked. This one rolled down quite low, which avoided the issue entirely. It was also one of their softest items of clothing.

After getting dressed, Hyde made sure the cats had fresh water and food. They gave Mortar a quick cuddle before setting them on the bed. It was early enough for them to enjoy the stillness of South Myrddin before most people were up and about.

Grabbing the They and Hello pins, Hyde added them to the top of their waistcoat, grinning so widely their fangs showed. The sun wouldn't rise for another hour or two, so they enjoyed the quiet walk through the village. The lamps flickered merrily, and little friendly flames bounced amongst the shadows.

Since the coffee shop Roasted and Toasted wouldn't be open for another thirty minutes, Hyde wandered in the opposite direction, heading down Harbour Road.

None of the shops were open yet. They inspected the window array in Unclouded Light—the jeweller. Aroha Kiri was a panther shifter from New Zealand who'd found her way to South Myrddin at fifteen. She made beautiful pieces of wearable art. Their Yule displays were always something special.

Continuing a little further down the lane, Hyde stopped outside The Den, the only boarding house in the village. It had originally been a country home, which lore held that South Myrddin had been built up around. Reuben Rutherford, the current owner, had purchased it when he arrived a year before them.

The tallest and strongest of any shifter or wolf in the village, Reuben, as a werewolf, was definitely the alpha of the village pack. He'd created The Den as a safe space for those without a home.

While werewolves and vampires didn't usually mix well, Hyde had always found a friend in the man. To them, at least, Reuben was a gentle giant. They knew he had the potential to be otherwise when threatened.

"Up early, little cub." Reuben came out of the house with a wooden crate in hand. He set it beside a ladder that was leaning to the right of the door. "Want to give me a hand with putting up lights for Yule?"

"Because I'm so much taller than you?" Hyde peered up at him by way of demonstration.

"Don't get mouthy." He chuckled when they smiled wide enough to give him a full few of their fangs. "How about you just feed me the string of lights so I can set them up?"

"Not sure Dr Wilfred would approve of you eating lights." Hyde paused for a brief moment. "You didn't mean actually eat. Right. We'll pretend this part of the conversation never happened."

Between the two of them, they managed to get the lights strung up above the front first-floor windows and the door. Hyde left him to it and retraced their steps back down the lane. The siren call of caffeine could no longer be ignored.

Roasted and Toasted, like most places in the village, had a quaint feel to it, from the aged stone to the ivy creeping up along the side. Hyde peered through one of the large windows to find Shikoba already busy behind the counter. They headed inside, greeted by the beautiful smells of coffee and baked goods.

Shikoba Apanni had come to the village several years earlier. They were originally from Louisiana and the Choctaw Nation. As a two-spirited eagle shifter, they'd been on the hunt for a place to make home and settled on South Myrddin.

"Who are we this morning?"

Hyde pointed to the badge on their waistcoat. "An uncaffeinated they."

"Uncaffeinated is a problem I can solve." Shikoba had their long raven-black hair tied up in a loose bun that seemed to defy the laws of gravity. Their air of calm had always been something Hyde envied. "Up early, are we?"

"Two cats and a witch made for a snoring chorus." Hyde happily accepted a tiny mug with a tiny taste of one of their new blends. They sniffed the coffee carefully. "Cinnamon and chocolate?"

"I'm calling it the Vega blend for Teresa. It's cinnamon, coffee, and an unsweetened cocoa mixed with my own sweet syrup concoction. A spiced mocha, if you like. I've got brown butter iced chocolate cinnamon rolls to go with them. There's also an orange and cranberry scone if you want something slightly less sweet."

Hyde finished the little mug of coffee. "I've a feeling it's going to be a trying day. Just... something in the air. Can we have two large Vega...? That sounds wrong. Two large coffees plus two scones and two cinnamon rolls?"

"Sure." Shikoba busied themselves getting the order together. "Looks chilly outside. Might be a good day."

"I hope so." Hyde couldn't shake the ominous feeling that had begun to settle on them. "I do."

"Here. I've included a few extra biscuits. Cheer yourself up." Shikoba reached out to give their hand the gentlest of touches. "Whatever the wind brings in on it, you're not alone in handling it."

"Not... comforting, Shikoba. Not comforting."

Shikoba came around the counter. They brought their hands up, murmuring under their breath in Choctaw. "Everything happens as it should, Hyde. You'll be fine."

Time seemed to slow for the briefest of moments. Hyde had no idea how long they'd been standing in the coffee shop. It had definitely been more than a few minutes.

"Mildly more comforting. Yakoke." Hyde used one of the few Choctaw words they'd learned—the one for thank you. They paid for the breakfast and coffee once Shikoba returned to their spot behind the counter, stacked the two cups on top of the box, and made their way slowly across the lane towards the bookshop.

"What the Dickens are they doing here?"

Three familiar figures stood outside the bookshop. Hyde tightly grasped the box of pastries and coffee to keep from dropping them. Detective Chief Inspector Jonatan Pacheco appeared to be in mid-argument with two members of the Snodgrass family. They immediately recoiled as panic rushed through them and considered turning around and walking until they were out of the village just to avoid the confrontation.

"Hello, Hy—" Eunice started, seeming surprised but perhaps happy to see them. It was always so hard to read other people's emotions.

"It's Hyde. People who abandon children don't get to stamp their mark on them." They interrupted their aunt, unsure if she was aware of their name change. They had chosen it from a book. It sounded phonetically pleasing to them. "I took the surname. It's mine. You can't have it back."

"Thank you for telling me, Hyde. I was never told you changed it. We would like to speak with you." Eunice Snodgrass sounded sincere, but Hyde could never tell. She'd married into the family to their loathsome uncle Magnus. "Could we step inside your lovely bookshop?"

Hyde didn't know what to say to their aunt, so they turned to Magnus instead. "You helped someone attempt to kill me over a book. Why are you here?"

"To mend fences." He seemed far less sincere than his wife.

"I don't have any fences. I have a shop—and you're not welcome in it." Hyde stepped around them, continuing on to where Teresa waited, having come outside. "Why are they here?"

"No idea." Teresa pushed the door open and closed it firmly once they were both inside. "Pacheco's been arguing with them for a few minutes, trying to get them to leave."

Hyde set the coffee and box of treats on the counter. They scrubbed their fingers roughly over their face. "I honestly thought I'd never have to deal with them again until Enzo Bassani mentioned Magnus."

Enzo Bassani had murdered his own son and tried to frame his daughter Amalia. In the process, he'd claimed to have worked a deal out with Magnus Snodgrass to steal the family journal, a version of a grimoire, from Hyde and kill them. There had only been his word and no actual proof. It was odd to see them in the village now after everything.

Hyde tensed when the door to the shop opened. They were oddly relieved to see DCI Pacheco and not Magnus or Eunice. "What the dickens are they doing here?"

"They came to apologise."

Jonatan Pacheco had the dubious honour of being one the eldest and strongest vampires in Scotland—probably the world. He was the coven leader for the region and took his role incredibly seriously. His somewhat autocratic manner had always grated on Hyde. Their relationship had been rocky from the start but had recently begun to soften.

Hyde shook their head slowly, trying to process what Pacheco had said. "The Snodgrasses don't do that."

"You do. And they're your family."

"No, no, they're not. This village? That's my family. I only have the misfortune of sharing blood and a name with the Snodgrasses," Hyde stated firmly.

"I suppose you're not wrong." Pacheco seemed as frustrated as Hyde. "I have no idea why they're in the village with their son."

"Son? Phineas is here?" Hyde had nothing negative to say about their cousin. He'd been kind to them when they were younger. "Odd. He's never been close to his parents."

"I am loath to make accusations without evidence." Pacheco took his job as detective chief inspector as seriously as he did as a coven leader. He'd dug into Enzo Bassani's accusations but came up with nothing concrete enough to make an arrest. "Please be cautious around them. I've encouraged them to leave."

"And?" Teresa asked while Hyde stared moodily down at the pastries.

"The very first attempt they make to harass you, I will force the issue. I have no reason to do so at this moment." He hesitated before turning to leave. "I am trying to be a good coven leader—for all of the vampires and not just those with supposed power and status."

They watched Pacheco leave the shop in silence. Hyde glanced over at Teresa, who shrugged. They could see through the new stained-glass windows as he once again engaged the Snodgrasses in conversation, leading them away from the shop.

"Odd."

"Distinctly," Hyde agreed.

"Maybe he took what happened to heart?" Teresa snagged one of the cups of coffee. "Oh, this is delicious."

"The Vega blend."

"What?" She coughed a few times to clear her throat. "Vega blend?"

"Shikoba says it was inspired by you—and your Mexican side."

"Brilliant. I wonder if I can get a cut off the profits." Teresa grinned.

"We did get some free biscuits."

The rest of the day passed relatively calmly. Hyde stayed in their shop with Mortar and Pestle being a little proactive in assessing who came inside. They deterred anyone who might disrupt their calm.

Thankfully for all of them, the Snodgrasses had

chosen to stay away. Hyde didn't think their family was done with them. They just wished the three would go away and never come back.

Hyde cuddled Mortar and Pestle in their arms. "Here's hoping we have a quiet night."

4

TERESA

A SHRILL SCREAM JOLTED TERESA AWAKE. She'd spent much of the evening giving the kitchen on the first floor of the bus a thorough clean and prepping for the morning. It had been one of those evenings when Hyde had lost themselves in a book, so she gave them space.

By the time a second scream rent the air, Teresa had bolted out of bed. She threw on jeans and a T-shirt, managing to shove on a pair of shoes without taking a header down the narrow stairs of the bus. Her coat was hanging by the door, so she grabbed it on the way out to keep from freezing.

Teresa spotted a hysterical Eunice being held by a younger vampire. *Shite.*

Thankfully, the light from the lamps was bright

enough to give her a clear view. Teresa could see an odd mound to the left of the bookshop's front door. She inched closer, trying to avoid the attention of the two vampires.

There appeared to be a large pile of ash. It was the clothing that truly caught her attention—a full three-piece suit complete with shoes, leather gloves, and several pieces of very expensive jewellery. Teresa frowned at the dark turquoise suit jacket with copper buttons. She'd seen it somewhere.

Oh, bollocks.

Teresa had a sinking feeling she was staring at the remnants of Magnus Snodgrass. He had clearly died on Hyde's doorstep.

This is going to be an absolute nightmare.

As if summoned by her thoughts, Hyde opened the door. Their gaze darted from Teresa to the ashes to the rest of their family. Teresa thought they were probably tempted to return to the shop and ignore everything.

Eunice screamed again. Her son dragged her away from the scene. It gave them all a second to process what was happening.

Hyde hadn't moved from the front of the shop. "Ashes to ashes."

"Hyde." Teresa stepped around the pile of ash,

clothing, jewellery, and what appeared to be a greenish-brown powder amidst the grey. "Why don't we step back into the bookshop?"

The screeching from Eunice had reached an excruciatingly high pitch. A sharp whistle thankfully cut through everything. Teresa was relieved to see DCI Pacheco striding towards them, which was a surprising change from the feeling he usually engendered.

For the longest time, Pacheco had been almost like the overly strict teacher everyone not so secretly loathed. He'd mellowed within the past month or so. Teresa wondered if being forced to face his actions, or lack thereof, when it came to some of the vampires within the coven had made him reassess his approach.

Pacheco finally reached them. His attention immediately went to the pile of ash and clothing on the ground. It was easy to see he recognised it for what it was. He pulled out his phone and sent a message before approaching them. "Has anyone touched anything?"

"No. I kept Mother from touching it. No one else did." Phineas spoke up. He'd, by some miracle, managed to settle Eunice. He dragged his fingers through his ginger curls. They reminded Teresa of

Hyde's hair, though cut slightly differently. "Father—"

"I'll ask questions of you in a moment." Pacheco held a hand up to stop him. "Separately. Why don't you lead Eunice to my car? She can sit in the back and regain her composure."

Teresa stayed by Hyde's side. They watched as the Constables Jain arrived together. "Here comes trouble."

The Jain twins, Trishna and Vidya, had moved to South Myrddin from Bengaluru after trouble with their family. They'd become constables a few years back. Teresa enjoyed the two of them.

Detective Inspector Fynn Baines arrived not long after. He appeared to have come straight from home. His long dreadlocks were down where he usually kept them pulled back when working. It hid the tattoo on his neck and the seer mark on his left temple. "What happened?"

"A dead vampire," Hyde muttered before anyone else could answer. They shrugged when everyone glanced at them. "Am I wrong?"

Fynn stepped over to Pacheco. He pulled two pairs of gloves out of his pocket, offering one to his boss. "Any idea who he is?"

"Magnus Snodgrass." Pacheco knelt down. He

asked Vitya to grab him several evidence bags and call the forensic scene examiner. His attention seemed drawn to the greenish-brown powder Teresa had noticed. "I know this. Phyllan pyr. A sacred leaf used by druids in many rituals. It happens to be deadly, in a dried and powdered form, to vampires if ingested."

Druids.

There were several in South Myrddin. Teresa glanced at Hyde. She had no doubts they were both assuming Pacheco would immediately consider Emrys a suspect.

The vampire and druid had a history that no one ever talked about. They were often antagonistic towards each other. They had very different ideas on how best to protect the village, foundlings, and Hyde, in particular.

"Mother." Phineas was chasing after Eunice, who'd left the solitude of Pacheco's vehicle. She stormed down the pavement. "Mother. Stop."

Eunice pointed towards Emrys, who had appeared as if summoned, walking up the lane and towards the bookshop. "Druid's work. He did it."

"Be careful where you point fingers." Emrys simply raised an eyebrow at her. His attention turned to the pile of dust. "Magnus Snodgrass, I presume?"

"Why don't we speak?" Pacheco stood back up. He handed the evidence packet to Fynn and moved away from the others with Emrys following.

With a muttered curse, Teresa watched the conversation unfold from a distance. She had no doubts the vampires could probably eavesdrop on it. They had far superior hearing. Hyde, as an autistic, had especially sensitive ears.

Teresa tried to grab Hyde, but they easily slipped out of her grasp. *Bollocks.*

Hyde stormed over to where Pacheco was heatedly questioning Emrys. "He didn't do it."

"I think you underestimate what Emrys would do for someone he loves." Pacheco had an almost bittersweet look on his face. "It's those he's indifferent to that he prefers to ignore entirely."

"I wasn't... I am not indifferent."

"How'd you get here so quickly?" Hyde interrupted, staring pointedly at Pacheco. "It's a longer drive than it took you."

"I was sorting out my differences with Emrys when Phineas sent me a message."

Teresa exchanged a confused look with Hyde. "Sorting out your differences?"

"You two stay out of this investigation. I mean it. You've gotten your nose into two murder inquiries.

Do not touch this one, particularly you." Pacheco pointed to Hyde. "You wouldn't harm a fly. I have no doubts about that. But you know what your family is like. They'll start asking if you were involved. Please keep away from this for both our sakes."

"I didn't do anything to him. I didn't want anything to do with him or anyone else." Hyde glowered at him. "And I didn't poke my nose anywhere. I accidentally stumbled into two murder inquiries. Unintentionally."

"Unintentionally?"

"Jonatan." Emrys placed a hand on Pacheco's arm. "Why don't you invite me to speak with you somewhere more officially? I have nothing to hide. Can you say the same?"

Teresa leaned into Hyde, who'd been watching the brief exchange avidly. "Why does it feel like we're watching former lovers verbally spar?"

"Because we are?" Hyde whispered. They sounded just as bewildered. "What's happening?"

"A murder with a side quest of rekindled romance gone wrong?" Teresa tried not to laugh. It seemed inappropriate with the ashes of a vampire not far from them. "Should we walk away?"

"Yes, you should," Pacheco hissed sharply. "You should both go into the bookshop. Don't speak with anyone, particularly your aunt or cousin. Try not to disturb the ashes. Fynn will speak with you both once he finishes the scene."

"Why do I feel like our parents have sent us to our room without dessert?" Teresa asked as she guided Hyde towards the bookshop; they sidestepped the ashes, police, and their still mildly hysterical aunt. She waited until they were inside before speaking. "Are you okay?"

"I...." Hyde crouched down to lift Mortar into their arms. They buried their face in the cat's fluffy silvery-grey fur. "How am I supposed to feel? He was an absolutely dreadful person."

"He was."

"He tried to kill me."

Teresa once again nodded her agreement. "He did."

"So, why am I sad? *Am* I sad?"

"Because family is complicated? And some part of you may always wish they'd treated you like you mattered?" Teresa sidled up to them. She looped her arm around Hyde's back. "It's perfectly okay to be sad —or not. You feel what you feel."

5

HYDE

"You feel what you feel."

The trouble was that Hyde rarely knew exactly what was going on emotionally inside them. They often struggled to identify feelings accurately. Magnus had been a horrible vampire, but they didn't know how to process his death.

His murder.

The shop was eerily quiet for late morning. It had taken the police several hours to process the scene. Hyde tried not to find their having to sweep up the ashes amusing. It was in a macabre sort of way.

"Is it fitting that a vampire who spent his entire life feeling superior was in death swept up with a broom?" Hyde sipped tea that Teresa had made for

them. "I know they gathered up the evidence first. But in the end, it was just a broom."

"Just a broom sweeping up the dirt?"

Hyde snorted into the mug of tea. "Should I be laughing at that? I shouldn't."

"No one in this room is going to judge you." Teresa came over to stand by the windows with them. "I wonder where Eunice and Phineas went."

"Far away from here, I hope." Hyde figured they'd probably been taken to the nearest police station. "Fynn never did come to ask questions."

"You spoke too soon." Teresa pointed to where they could see Fynn making his way towards the door. He stepped into Between the Leaves, waving at them and crouching down to pick up Pestle, who'd flounced over to greet him. "Detective Inspector."

"Teresa. Jekyll." Fynn gently set Pestle on the counter and then turned his attention to them. "What can you tell me?"

Only a handful of people referred to Hyde as Jekyll. It had been a nickname Fynn started when they were a much younger vampire. It always made them smile.

"Jekyll?" Fynn prompted when they hadn't said anything. "Talk to me about last night or this morning? What did you see?"

"Nothing." Hyde shrugged. "I had no interactions with Magnus Snodgrass except when the entire group was outside the shop early in the day yesterday. I've no idea how he came to be a pile of ash and cloth in front of my door. None of it makes sense—particularly them being in South Myrddin."

"What alerted you to something being wrong?"

"Eunice's screeching. Actually, Mortar woke me up, and then I heard the sound." Hyde still found the entire thing odd, from the death to the reaction of her aunt.

"How was Eunice behaving when you saw her?" Fynn had pulled his notebook out of his pocket.

"Aside from hysterical?" Teresa offered.

"Screaming like a banshee." Hyde set their empty mug on the counter with a sigh. They went around the counter and bent down to hunt for a bag of treats for the cats. "It's odd. Eunice has always been the picture of poise. I've never heard her raise her voice. Though it's been close to a century since I've seen her, so I suppose people can change."

"Maybe it was the shock of seeing her husband turned to ash." Fynn jotted something down in his notebook. "I've seen grief do all manner of things to people. How about Phineas? Their son."

"Quiet. From what I remember, it is his usual

state of being." Hyde had only a few memories of their cousin. He'd always kept to himself. "Mild-mannered. But again, it's been years since I last saw him. People can change as they get older."

"It's always the quiet ones." Teresa did a lousy job of hiding her smile behind her mug.

"I'm a quiet one," Hyde grumbled.

"Except you."

"Anything else you remember?" Fynn drew them back to the matter at hand.

"Aside from Magnus Snodgrass being a terrible individual? No." Teresa seemed utterly unrepentant when Fynn glanced at her. "Am I wrong?"

"She's not wrong." Hyde had mostly negative memories of Magnus. "He did give Enzo Bassani everything he needed to kill me."

"If only we could've proved it." Fynn tapped his pen against the notebook. He finally closed the book and put both away in his pocket. "How are you taking all of this?"

"I...." Hyde held their hands up, struggling to find any sort of explanation. "Apathy. Relief. A faint tinge of something resembling sadness."

"Do you know who could've done this?" Fynn asked after a few moments of silence.

Hyde thought about Emrys and Bram. They'd

both go to great lengths to protect any foundling in the village from threat. Their mind went to DCI Pacheco, who, despite everything, also had the capability of it. "Not really."

"Hyde."

"I was sound asleep with the cats," they insisted.

"Vampires don't require sleep."

"I don't require a lot of things, but I enjoy them anyway. I don't *require* these chocolate biscuits, but I'm still going to devour one." Hyde tossed the entire thing into their mouth. They chewed slowly while Fynn sighed. "I'm still in the second stage of my life. I've got another half a century or more before I age up again. Maybe I'll get grey hair."

Vampires tended to age incredibly slowly. The first stage took them through childhood into what visually appeared to be their teen years. Hyde had aged in appearance to somewhere in their thirties. It was certainly better than appearing as a child for an eternity.

A vampire rarely died of natural causes. Accidents or murders were usually what ended their lives. Hyde hoped to avoid either. Their uncle had clearly not been so lucky.

"Maybe this is hypocritical of me because I've encouraged you to use your clever mind in investigations." Fynn took a step closer. He ran his fingers through Pestle's fur. "Stay away from the investigation. Please. It involves your uncle. A family you're estranged from. None of which is your fault, but the smartest thing you can do is avoid even coming close to the murder inquiry. Okay?"

"I wasn't trying to get involved in the other ones. They fell in my lap. Not literally," Hyde grumbled. "Well, almost."

"Please be careful." Fynn asked them a few more questions before leaving the shop.

Once Fynn had left, Hyde felt like they were suffocating in the shop. They tried to shake off the sensation, but nothing helped. Once Teresa went back to the taco bus to prep for the day, they ducked out of the bookshop for a walk alone.

They made their way through Raven Park, past the ritual circle, towards the shore. Loch Bard was particularly stormy. The wind whipped up the waves. The chaotic power spoke to Hyde's mood more than anything else.

As Hyde often had as a young vampire, they found their way to a large rock midway between the village and the lighthouse. It was usually a peaceful place, off the usual footpath around the loch. They climbed on top, got comfortable, and watched the waves batter the shore.

Closing their eyes, Hyde tried to sift through the chaotic silence in their brain. The thoughts floated out of reach in the quiet numbness. They weren't sure how to identify the emotions bubbling up inside.

A sound drew them out of their thoughts. Hyde listened to the cadence of the steps. They had no doubts about who it was.

"Emrys."

"Hello, foundling." Emrys joined them on the rock. He pulled out his favourite pipe, one that had a dragon carved into the wood. It completed his look of a weathered fisherman with his slightly untamed shoulder-length grey hair and his beard. The scent reminded her of being a young vampire and following him around the village. "Water is unsettled."

Hyde nodded, watching as the wind blew the waves and they aggressively crashed onto the shore. "Water isn't the only unsettled thing in the village."

"Do you want to talk about it?"

Hyde shrugged. They hadn't figured out how to find words to address their complex and confused emotions. "Did you do it?"

"I did not." Emrys puffed out intricate smoke rings. "I know how it was done but not by whom."

"Why would someone kill him outside my shop?"

"I'm not sure. To attempt to frame you? Or me?" Emrys tapped his fingers against his pipe. "I haven't the foggiest idea. I wouldn't do that to you, foundling. I wouldn't sully the village earth with murder."

"No, you'd do it outside the village if you thought it would protect us." Hyde was mostly joking. They sighed again, leaning against Emrys's side. "Why did they come here? Why now?"

"Magnus failed to retrieve the Snodgrass journal through Enzo Bassani. It's possible he decided to take matters into his own hands." Emrys made sure to blow his smoke rings so the wind carried them away. "Did you ever discover who sent it to you in the first place?"

"We had a few suspicions. Pacheco thought maybe an aunt. I'm not sure." Hyde stared morosely out at the choppy water. "Should I mourn him?"

"Not sure this is a situation with a right or wrong answer. Grief is a tricky beast."

"I'm not happy that he died." They contemplated the smoke rings floating away on the wind for a few moments. "I'm not sad either. I don't feel anything aside from maybe guilt that I *should* have some sort of emotion over his murder."

"Your family abandoned you. We believe Magnus attempted to have you killed, though Jonatan claims the police can't prove it." Emrys repeated what they'd already thought themselves. "You don't owe anyone your grief, foundling. I wouldn't blame you if you wanted to dance in his ashes."

"Emrys."

"He hasn't earned your dirge, so don't feel compelled to hum so much as a bar of the lament." Emrys puffed on his pipe for a moment. "Do you want to hide in my library? You haven't been there in a while."

Hyde hesitated. "Pacheco would say one shouldn't run from their problems."

"There's no shame in wanting time and space to process what's happened without people asking questions. My library is always a safe place for you." Emrys carefully slipped off the rock and waited for them. "And Jonatan has run from his fair share of troubles over the centuries."

"Like?" Hyde couldn't help asking.

"Never you mind."

The walk to Emry's home didn't take long. Hyde

was grateful he never minded silence. They weren't in the mood for conversation.

At the back of the garden stood a stone shed with a thatch roof. It had at one time been the original cottage. The inside had been completely gutted and then redone with floor-to-ceiling bookshelves. Climbing hydrangea covered almost the entire left side of the structure.

It had been Hyde's favourite place in the entire village as a young vampire. The shelves were filled with a mixture of first-edition novels and reference books. They'd often retreated inside when the world seemed far too large.

A single leather armchair sat in the corner of the room with soft, weathered quilts draped over it. Hyde hadn't visited in a while. They'd made their own book haven in the form of Between the Leaves.

Hyde ran their fingers along the spines of some of the books. "I always loved the secret library in your garden. It felt like a magical space—something out of one of the stories I'd read."

Emrys wandered over to the small table where a record player sat. He flicked through his stack of albums before choosing one. "I'll make some tea for you."

It was seconds before the familiar strains of classical music began playing—an album by Mermaid's Lament. The music was soft and moody. No heavy beat of drums, just a soothing yet sad melody to carry them away. Hyde sank into the armchair and closed their eyes, allowing the sound to wash over them.

Magnus was dead.

Hyde couldn't help wondering why now, and why in front of their shop.

What a wonderfully merry, murderous midwinter we're about to have.

6

TERESA

THE LONGER THE MORNING DRAGGED ON, THE more concerned Teresa grew. Hyde had yet to return from their walk. She worried about them being accosted by the remaining Snodgrasses.

It was past noon when a merlin falcon landed on the bus's open window. Teresa frowned before spotting a note tied to its leg. She reached out cautiously and retrieved it. The bird eyed her beadily before launching itself into flight.

"The foundling is resting in my garden. I shall take good care of them." Teresa read the note in Emrys's fluid script. She tucked it into her back pocket, feeling relieved. *Emrys and his merlins. Why are druids always so incredibly overdramatic?*

After another hour of serving tacos, Teresa took a

break to check on the cats. She darted over to the bookshop. They were snuggled up together in the armchair closest to the fire.

"Hello, lovelies." Teresa smiled when they completely ignored her. She held up the little bowl in her hand. "I've brought you a treat."

Mortar lazily opened her eyes. She lifted her head off Pestle's side. Both cats were only mildly interested as Teresa approached. They glanced towards the door.

"I'm sorry, chaos kitties. Hyde will be back soon, I promise." Teresa set the bowl on the chair beside them. "I'll check on you later—don't burn the shop down."

Mortar narrowed her eyes and hissed at Teresa, obviously offended by the insinuation. She chuckled as she made her way towards the front door. The cats were finicky beasts, particularly when Hyde wasn't around.

Teresa stepped out of the shop, glancing back to make sure the door was shut. She walked straight into someone. "Oh. Sorry."

"You. You're the girlfriend," Phineas stammered. He dragged his hand over his face, shaking his head. "Hyde's. For Dracul's sake. You are Hyde's girlfriend. Person. Person friend. Person. Friend."

"That's me. Their person friend." Teresa found herself strongly reminded of Hyde. "They're not in the shop at the moment if you're looking for them."

"Ah. Well. Right." Phineas's gaze darted from the stained-glass windows to the spot where his father had perished. "I'll come back."

At any other time, Teresa would've found it charming. But murder had made her highly suspicious of everything and everyone—particularly of the Snodgrasses. She knew how they'd treated Hyde.

Teresa watched Phineas wander down the pavement. He seemed completely lost. *What are you up to?*

After a few moments, Teresa returned to the taco bus. The tiny kitchen was set up efficiently. It had taken months of trial and error before she had gotten everything situated. Years on, it ran like a well-oiled machine.

A well-oiled machine of one.

The lunch rush, as much as it ever was in their small village, flew by. Winter months were often tough on everyone in South Myrddin. They banded together. It helped that Teresa had no rent to pay. She owned her bus outright, and the village never charged her for parking by the bookshop.

It was a relief when Hyde finally reappeared.

They seemed visibly lighter than earlier in the morning. Time in Emrys's garden had clearly done them well.

"Hello. How's my vampire person friend?"

Hyde came up onto the bus when Teresa opened the doors. They frowned in obvious confusion. "Vampire person friend? What are you talking about?"

"Your cousin asked if I was your person friend. It was oddly... endearing." Teresa continued closing up her little food bus. She'd shut the windows and began clearing up the remaining food. "He was looking for you. Care for a taco? I have enough to make a single one with some of the blood chicken and pork sausage you love."

"I could eat." Hyde began gathering up dishes to place in the warm, soapy water by the sink. "Why did Phineas want to see me? Was he angry?"

"I haven't the foggiest." Teresa made quick work of whipping up a taco for Hyde and one for herself. She offered a plate to Hyde. "Why don't we have a nosh on these and then finish cleaning up? You can check on your furry fiends before we pop by The Spiked Cauldron. Maybe there's some gossip about the police investigation."

"Not sure we have to go to the pub to hear gossip. On the way here from Emrys's, I heard no less than three bits of information." Hyde finished the taco in three bites. They sighed happily. "Apparently, Flossie and Winnie went skinny-dipping again. They've been informed the Arctic plunge doesn't happen in Loch Bard in early December."

"Who informed them?"

"No idea. Also, DCI Pacheco and Emrys had what Magali described as a *massive* row about something. I'm guessing the police investigation." Hyde continued to list off increasingly absurd bits of village gossip. "The Lyalls were offended by one of the new members of the pack staying at The Den. They've refused to clean it."

"I'm sure Reuben is thrilled." Teresa could only imagine how messy a boarding house full of were-wolves could get. "They better make amends quickly."

Isla, Lileas, and Fiona Lyall were cousins. The three gruagach, or brownies, ran a cleaning company called Feather Duster. They did such good work that Hyde even trusted them in their bookshop.

The cousins all suffered from a hereditary illness. It was a close-guarded secret, but Teresa knew they often went to Emrys for tonics to help. Brownies could be tetchy at the best of times. She always treated them with the greatest respect. They were great fun, full of mischief until they felt insulted.

"I imagine Reuben's going to be paying a hefty price to fix the mess." Teresa stowed everything needing refrigeration away. She turned to find Hyde making quick work of the mass of dishes. "Nothing like vampire speed and strength to make cleaning up go in the blink of an eye."

"Uncle Magnus would be horrified. Oh, the indignities." Hyde mimicked their uncle's voice. "The bonfire's going in Raven Park. How about we walk through it before going to the pub?"

"A midwinter's walk?" Teresa finished clearing up her prep space as Hyde took care of the last of the dishes. They'd done her closing-up tasks in a remarkably short amount of time. "As your person-friend thing, I'm blushing at the insinuation."

Hyde leaned in closer to inspect her face. "No, you aren't."

Teresa patted her cheeks a few times. "Now I am."

"Definitely not the same thing. Let me check on the furry fiends. I'm sure they're annoyed with me for being gone all day. I'll have a quick shower and change. We can meet up in an hour?" Hyde was gone in a flash, leaving Teresa staring bemusedly after them.

It was going to be an early night for them. Hyde was probably going to want to retreat to their shop earlier rather than later after the day they'd had. Teresa gave the kitchen one last wipe down before locking the front door and heading upstairs.

Since the bus had a permanent spot beside Between the Leaves, Teresa had been lucky enough to get it connected to the village's water and other important systems. The upstairs was basically a tiny home complete with an altar for her witchery, a shower, and her bedroom.

The shower was tiny, but it had hot water, which mattered on cold, blustery days. The magically reinforced bus could withstand the occasionally harsh winters. When the rare extreme storm happened, she tended to hunker down in the bookshop with Hyde.

When Hyde reappeared over an hour later, Teresa couldn't help smiling. They were wearing one of their ugly holiday sweaters, made by one of the Skeleton Crew knitters. It had small Santas that slightly resembled Emrys, along with snowflakes all over it.

A few years back, the crew had done a December challenge. They'd all knitted the ugliest sweaters from various patterns they'd created. Hyde had claimed the Santa one, mostly because it made both them and Emrys giggle like small children.

"One of these days, we'll have to make Emrys one so he can match you." Teresa looped her arm around Hyde's. They began heading down the lane towards the park. She breathed in deeply, enjoying the crisp air and scent of spiced orange and cranberry from the various simmering cauldrons. "The village is extra magical this time of year."

Hyde reached up to adjust their knitted hat. Ginger curls peeked out from underneath it. "I smell chocolate orange cinnamon rolls."

"I sense a need to stop by The Golden Puff before we continue." Teresa slipped her hand into Hyde's, then jogged across the lane to the bakery. "Surprised Rosa is open so late."

"She's always open late at least once a week like I am for the nocturnal visitors." Hyde pressed their face against the glass. "Oh. She's made her spiced blackberry and ginger pastries as well."

Rosa Pacheco had come to South Myrddin before Hyde. Though she was related to DCI Pacheco, the two weren't close. Her bakery combined her Spanish heritage with other recipes for a myriad of delicious treats.

Of all the vampires in the area, Rosa was the only one who seemed to understand Hyde. The two certainly got on better than the others. It helped that neither had joined the local coven.

Stepping into The Golden Puff, her senses were immediately assaulted by a delicate combination of spices, sweet, sugary bliss, and the divine mix of fruit and chocolate. Teresa was almost carried away by it. Hyde excitedly inspected all the goods Rosa had laid out in the various baskets and trays.

"This is always the best time of year." Hyde wiped the faceprint off the glass with their sleeve. They dragged Teresa towards the counter, where a bemused Rosa waited for them. "I smell cinnamon rolls."

"I've saved you the best one." Rosa placed two small boxes on the counter, sliding them towards them. "There's also a ginger blackberry tea. It'll keep you warm. Or it'll keep Teresa warm."

"I get cold," Hyde grumbled.

"That's because you are a wonderfully unique vampire." Rosa finished making up the teas for them. She set the two cups beside the boxes. "Here you go. Will I see you at the pub later? I'm closing in an hour or so."

"We'll be there," Teresa promised. They'd already lost Hyde to their cinnamon roll. "Seriously?"

"What?" Hyde blinked innocently. They smiled,

revealing fangs covered in the cinnamon sugar paste from the pastry. "Something wrong?"

"It is sometimes very hard to take you seriously as a vampire." Rosa took the payment for their treats, sneaking an extra bag of off-cut biscuits into Hyde's box. "Off you go."

Hyde considered her for a moment. "I'd hate to be taken seriously as anything other than a lover of books and cats. Oh, and Resa."

Teresa leaned into them, smiling mischievously. "And I am a lover of books, cats, and you."

"And tacos. We can't forget those," Rosa teased. "Go on. Away with you."

7

HYDE

Hyde sipped their tea while standing on the pavement. They'd already inhaled the cinnamon roll, leaving the box behind and stuffing the packet of biscuits into their coat pocket. "Outside of autumnal splendour, this might be my favourite time of year."

"Because of the treats?" Teresa gently wiped a speck of the frosting from their chin.

Grumbling under their breath, Hyde scrubbed at their chin with the sleeve of their sweater. They crouched down by a parked vehicle to check their reflection. It was going to drive them up the wall, thinking something was still on their face.

"Not just the treats." Hyde tilted their head to peer up at the garlands wrapped around the lampposts. "The decorations. The music. All of it. The way the

village smells like citrus, herbs, and spices. The lights glow a little brighter."

"You might say it's a magical time of year?" Teresa grinned when Hyde groaned audibly. "Am I wrong?"

"Yes. And no." Hyde slipped their hand into Teresa's, using their other to hold the cup of tea. "Are we decorating Guac-A-Mole again?"

For the past few years, Hyde and Teresa had coordinated the Yule decorations for the midwinter festival. The vintage double-decker bus lent itself well to a merry spruce-up. It was something they enjoyed doing together.

"I don't see why not. I still have all the lights."

"Don't call them faerie lights around Bram. He'll lecture you on the history of it." Hyde knew the fae took great delight in being as obnoxious as possible when it came to certain things. "You know what I hate about this time of year?"

"I have no idea." Teresa didn't even blink at the sudden change of topic.

Hyde always appreciated how Teresa rolled with their eccentricities. "The way small talk is even more difficult. How many ways can I say how dark it suddenly is, even when this happens every single year? I can only comment on how blustery and cold the weather is so much. Why can't people have real conversations?"

"Do you honestly want a real conversation with some people?" Teresa was silent for a moment before starting to chuckle quietly. "Just imagining a less superficial chat with DCI Pacheco."

"No, thank you. I've had enough of those to last me at least a century." Hyde could acknowledge the vampire coven leader had been attempting to change. It was hard to forget his autocratic and condescending tone from the recent past. "I'm not going to be good company tonight."

"Hyde."

They shook their head a few times. "I'm all over the place. My mind keeps bouncing from one thing to another. Feels like my brain is a spinning top, twirling about with no clear focus."

"Not the end of the world. How about we stroll through the park? Enjoy the bonfire and simmering cauldrons before I walk you home? You can have a quiet evening with the cats and a good book." Teresa always made it seem so simple and reasonable. "The last few days or so have been chaotic enough for anyone."

"But especially me?"

"It's done a job on my anxiety as well. You're not alone in feeling a confused array of emotions."

Though it made Hyde feel mildly better, they still struggled with not just pushing through. The closer they got to the park, the sounds of cheerful voices and music became louder. They immediately knew Teresa was right. It was not going to be a pub evening for them.

The Spiked Cauldron had a lovely, warm, and vibrant atmosphere most nights. It was one of the older buildings in the village and wouldn't have seemed out of place in a movie set in the eighteenth century. Dark, cosy, and occasionally cramped, depending on the number of patrons.

"I don't think it's going to be a pub night."

"That's all right." Teresa took a sip of her tea, guiding them down one of the paths into Raven Park. "Want to grab a takeaway from Wok Away or the Malt Moon? I'm fairly certain they're open for another hour or two. And you know Rees would make you a meal even if he'd already closed up."

"True." Hyde closed their eyes. They dragged the beanie down to cover their ears and tried to claw back the out-of-control sensation prickling under their skin. "I want to walk in the park and enjoy the start of the festivities. They'll have the mulled blood wine. And treats. And happy things."

"Park isn't going anywhere, love. We have days and days of the midwinter festival to come." Teresa stayed by their side, guiding them to a more secluded part of the park away from the various clumps of people. "It'll all still be here tomorrow. We can have a quiet night in at the bookshop—or you can have one on your own if you need."

"They—"

A shout drew both of their attention. They turned to see Emrys and Wilfred in the middle of an argument with DI Baines and DCI Pacheco. Wilfred Aniston was the village doctor and a druid. He was definitely not his usual calm self.

"What's going on?" Hyde kept their voice low. Teresa shrugged but followed willingly when they walked towards the raised voices. They caught sight of another druid, Hamish, who was a local paramedic, and joined him. "Something wrong?"

"The police want to ask Emrys a few questions." Hamish nodded towards the two druids. "Wilf's taken a bit of umbrage about it."

Taking Teresa by the hand, Hyde inched closer to the standoff between the police and the druids. They tried to get near enough to hear without involving themselves directly in what was thus far a mild confrontation. Emrys almost seemed to be taunting Pacheco, something they found incredibly odd.

"We just have a few questions." Fynn sounded as though he'd repeated himself multiple times.

"Ask him."

"We're not asking him questions about a murder in the middle of the park." Fynn tended to be rather calm, but he'd definitely reached the end of his tether.

"You think he did it." Wilfred stepped in front of Emrys and pointed accusingly at Pacheco. "Is this because he broke up with you over a century ago?"

"He didn't break up with me. I ended our... arrangement," Pacheco hissed quietly, though Hyde knew any of the vampires, shifters, and werewolves in the area had probably heard him. "This has nothing to do with ancient history. Magnus Snodgrass died under suspicious circumstances from ingesting a powdered herb known to be a druid speciality. It is only natural for us to question anyone who has knowledge about it. And Emrys is *The Druid*."

Hyde exchanged a wide-eyed look with Teresa, mouthing the words "Broke up" to her. They narrowed their eyes at the rest of Pacheco's statement. "You do think he did it."

"I have made zero assumptions." Pacheco towered over them. He gestured towards Emrys, who still seemed more amused than anything else. "We're going to ask him questions. Is everyone finished telling me how to do my job as the detective chief inspector, or can we proceed with our inquiry?"

Hyde went to open their mouth, then stopped when Pacheco pinched the bridge of his nose and sighed. "Emrys didn't kill Magnus."

"He knows more about phyllan par than anyone else in Scotland, maybe even the world." Pacheco turned towards Emrys, gesturing towards the path leading out of the park. "Shall we?"

"So much effort to ask me on a date." Emrys smirked in the face of Pacheco's aggravation. He patted Hyde on the shoulder lightly. "I'll be fine, foundling. There's no need for concern."

Following from a distance, Hyde looped their arm around Teresa's. They could do nothing but watch them drive off. It seemed a fell omen for what was supposed to be a joyous season.

"Are you concerned? Because I'm quite worried." Hyde found their early chaotic mind had focused on one thing—anxiety over Emrys. "I think it's time to have a conversation with *Auntie* Eunice."

"I'd wager you've never called her that in your entire life."

"I've never called her much of anything. I don't honestly recall spending much time with her before they banished me." Hyde added a dramatic tone to the end, trying to make light of something horrible. "She was always standoffish to my memory."

"And Phineas?"

"An odd duck, like me." Hyde made their way out of the park. Any lingering remnants of wanting to be festive had vanished entirely. Teresa kept pace with them. "I want to know why they came to South Myrddin."

"The grimoire?"

"Magnus's motive, sure. But why all three of them? Wouldn't he have wanted to keep his dealings close to his chest? The Snodgrasses, as a whole, are a viper's den with a meticulously created façade of beauty and propriety." Hyde still had the unnerving electric feeling of a postponed shutdown or meltdown under their skin. "Maybe we can track them down in the morning."

"Not tonight?"

"Tonight is a comfort night. Pyjamas. Heavy blankets. The cats. A marathon of *Law and Disorder: Druids and Warlocks.*" Hyde knew it was one way to slowly bleed off the sensation and help their mind calm itself. "Might work on that ancient Greek manuscript Magali asked me to translate for her."

"She'll be excited. How about I grab us some snacks?" Teresa left them at the door of the bookshop and wandered off to procure something for them to nosh on.

Stepping into the bookshop, Hyde allowed some of the tension to fall away. The protections Emrys had worked around the shop always drifted over their body like a warm embrace when they stepped into the building. Between the Leaves was their home— and it welcomed them.

Mortar rose from the bed by the fireplace with a graceful stretch while Pestle tumbled headfirst out of his. The ginger cat shook himself and then sauntered towards Hyde. Both of her chaos kitties trod lightly, as if they sensed the stress and tiredness.

Hyde hunted behind the counter for the Greek text. They enjoyed translating as a hobby. It wasn't done for pay, though villagers usually bartered with them for the service. "Ah. Found you."

Technically, it was a copy of a manuscript. There was no way Hyde would ever get their hands on the precious, crumbling original document. Magali had claimed she just wanted to know if a specific ritual was contained within.

In Hyde's experience, witches were always on the hunt for new potions, rituals, and spells. It was different, they supposed, from being a vampire, which never changed.

They had fangs, drank blood, and had exceptionally long lives and aged a few times over the centuries. There were a few other perks, sure, but no book or spell or potion would alter their existence.

"All right, upstairs we go." Hyde opened the door leading upstairs to their flat. Pestle raced ahead while Mortar followed close behind. "Home."

Home.

It always felt good to be within their own space. Hyde carefully lit the fire and a few candles. They dug in their wardrobe for their favourite pyjamas. A deep, rich burgundy shade, they were the softest things in existence. Magali had gifted them to them several years ago; they wore them on especially rough days.

After having a quick shower, Hyde was dressed and ensconced by the fire in a relatively short amount of time. Vampire speed occasionally made the dreary parts of life much easier. They dragged their heaviest blanket around their body. Mortar stretched out in their lap while Pestle lay to their left, watching the door for intruders.

A mass of pillows and blankets made for a comfortable seat in front of the coffee table. Hyde turned on the *Law and Disorder* marathon. It was one of their favourite comfort shows. They knew the first season almost by heart.

Leaning back against the couch behind them, Hyde closed their eyes. They let the familiar sounds wash over them. Their fingers drifted through Mortar's silky fur.

Minutes went by. Their shoulders slowly began to lower. Tension bled off bit by bit until they could fully formulate thoughts again.

"What do you think, Mortar? Why would they all come to South Myrddin?" Hyde sat up after a few more minutes. They took a deep breath, allowing their body to relax even further. "It's... so very odd."

8

TERESA

To her delight, Wok Away had been open. Evelyn and Lee Tham had come from Beijing a decade ago. They were fox shifters who served the best pot stickers in the world, in Teresa's opinion.

Evelyn boxed up all of Hyde's favourites and sent Teresa off. One of the best things about their little village was how everyone rallied around one another. It was important for everyone to feel welcomed and appreciated.

Something most hadn't experienced from their own covens or families.

Teresa made it halfway back to the bookshop when she ran into Magali and Maud in the midst of a debate. "Good evening."

"Tell her that we can't change the coven's

midwinter ritual at the eleventh hour." Maud gestured towards Magali.

"We can't change the coven's midwinter ritual at the eleventh hour," Teresa dutifully repeated with a wry grin on her face.

"And you tell her that change isn't going to cause the world to collapse," Magali hissed in obvious annoyance.

"Change—" Teresa was cut off by Maud swatting her on the arm. She decided to mediate the conflict between her fellow witch coven members instead of taking the mickey. "What's really going on here?"

Magali Porcher ran the local yarn shop, Woolly Witch. A born witch, Maud owned the Witching Hour, an antique shop. She'd been in the village for over twenty years. No one quite knew where she'd come from.

Maud glanced at Magali, who crossed her arms and huffed. "One of us has to take Florence's place on midwinter. And I thought, perhaps, Morrigan."

"And I think Flossie and Winnie should be the ones to decide."

The dynamics of the village witch coven tended to be occasionally spiky but mostly friendly. Florence, Flossie, and Winnie had always been the ones to lead it despite Teresa suspecting both Maud and Morrigan were arguably more powerful. They both appeared far younger than they were—not that she'd ever dare ask their age.

"We still have a few days." Teresa raised an eyebrow when both of the witches turned to glower at her. "Don't shoot the messenger. I'm stating facts. How about we see what happens on the day? We all know the ritual by heart; it's not as though any one of us couldn't take the lead without it causing an issue."

With one last glare, Maud went off in one direction, and Magali strode towards their shop. Teresa shook her head at the dramatics, chuckling to herself. She finally continued on herself, wanting to get back to Hyde before they started to worry.

There wasn't usually a leadership struggle within the Highlands' witch coven. Flossie, Winnie, and Florence had made a powerful triad of witches. With the death of the latter, it had started to become clear that the other two members of the trio were less interested in running everything.

Teresa made her way into the bookshop. She couldn't help smiling when she spotted Hyde in a mound of pillows and blankets in front of the telly with the cats around them. "Maud and Magali were arguing over who should lead the ritual on midwinter."

"Really? Coven drama days before Yule? Scandalous." Hyde gasped dramatically. They reached out for the paper bag from Wok Away. "They were open?"

"Evelyn stayed open a little later this evening. All your favourites." Teresa went into the kitchenette to retrieve plates, napkins, and chopsticks. Hyde had their own set, gifted by the Thams, since they struggled with the disposable wooden ones. Something about the texture set them off. "Not sure if it's official coven drama. They were being spiky with each other."

Hyde dug through the various containers inside the bag until they found the honey garlic roast spare ribs. "I do love their ribs."

"That's because they make the sauce with a hint of blood."

"Are you saying I'm bloody thirsty?" Hyde grinned widely, showing a hint of fang.

"You're horrible." Teresa flicked a cashew at them, laughing when Mortar batted it out of the air. "Saved by the queen feline herself."

"Thank you." Hyde gave Mortar a loving head rub.

"Feeling better?"

"Drained but better." Hyde deftly used their chopsticks to hunt for the perfect bit of rib.

"Was I hallucinating, or did Pacheco and Emrys basically confirm they used to date?" Teresa sat beside Hyde on the floor, setting the bottles of blood ale and regular ale on the coffee table. "They admitted it, right?"

"I think so." Hyde shifted closer, forcing an unhappy Mortar to move over a little. "Their 'arrangement.' A funny way of saying a romantic entanglement."

"I wonder what happened. There is certainly no love lost between them now." Teresa grabbed one of the containers of lo mein. It had been a long day, and she was starving. "And why was Pacheco so insistent that he ended it, not Emrys?"

"Vampires and druids don't historically get along. I imagine, particularly if this happened a century or two ago, Pacheco faced a lot of resistance from the elders in the coven. He's ambitious. Maybe he ended the relationship to keep his position." Hyde swapped the remainder of the ribs for the lo mein. "We know how much he cares about his reputation."

"Enough to break up with the love of his life?"

"It might explain why they've spent over a hundred years being narky with each other." Hyde settled back against the pillows.

A companionable silence fell between them.

Teresa knew after being overwhelmed, Hyde often needed time to recover. They finished the food while watching an episode of *Law & Disorder* that she was fairly certain they'd seen at least three times.

Teresa wasn't surprised when Hyde drifted off to sleep in the middle of the next episode. She glanced down at an inquisitive Pestle, who came over to sit in her lap. "Yes, your vampire does nap a lot for someone who doesn't need to sleep."

With a little effort, Teresa got Hyde situated more comfortably on the couch. She covered them with the blankets and cats, leaving the telly on for background noise. There were still a few things left to do at the taco bus, so she left them snoozing and headed out of the bookshop, making sure to lock up behind her.

"Ms Vega."

Teresa narrowed her eyes at the vampire who appeared in front of her. "You aren't welcome here. Hyde's busy."

"I am not the enemy here. My purpose in coming to South Myrddin was hoping to keep Magnus from hurting Hyde." Eunice sounded sincere enough. She placed her hands into the pockets of her expensive velvet coat. "Phineas joined me, wanting to reconcile with his cousin. I tried to tell him to stay at home, but he was quite insistent. Odd for him. He's never insistent on anything. Ah, well. Children. They never listen no matter their age."

"It's late. Bookshop is closed." Teresa didn't fancy her chances against the full strength of a vampire, but she'd take the risk for Hyde's sake if it came to it. "Why don't you come back tomorrow?"

"Vampires don't need rest."

"Neither do the wicked or the weary." Teresa waited for a moment, then started walking towards her bus.

"You love them."

Teresa paused to glance back over her shoulder only to find Eunice had vanished. "Blasted vampires. Not you, Hyde. You're brilliant."

The shop was silent. She listened to the music and voices coming up from the park. Melodies drifted on the wind, which whistled through the trees as a harmony

Teresa stood for several minutes until the chill started to sink into her. She strode towards the bus, putting vampires, murder, and festivals out of her mind for the moment. "A blessed almost Yule to us all. Here's hoping we make it through alive with all our bits intact."

9

HYDE

"What the dickens happened?" Hyde woke up groggy and confused. They blinked a few times before trying to sit up. Mortar yowled at them in aggravation before slinking off to join Pestle at the end of the couch on a mound of blankets. "What time is it?"

Since the universe didn't answer, Hyde dragged themselves up off the couch and discovered it was barely five in the morning. It was too early for most of the village to be up and about.

After having a luxuriously long bath, they dressed in one of their favourite vintage tweed suits, ruining the image slightly with one of their ugly holiday sweaters. This one had reindeer along with figures who bore striking resemblances to the various druids in the village. "All right, you two, why don't we open the bookshop early this morning? Make up for being shut mostly for the past few days?"

Mortar led the way down the stairs into the shop. Pestle followed close behind Hyde. The two cats meowed dramatically over the empty bowl in their corner. Hyde checked the drop-off box by the front door, where overnight deliveries were often left.

"Ah. Ada's books finally arrived." Hyde collected the two packages wrapped in brown paper and tied with twine. They glanced at the two cats, who'd finished their breakfast already. "You two behave yourselves while I swing by the orchard."

Ada Senft was a dryad who owned and worked the orchard on the outskirts of the village. She was also incredibly gifted with woodcraft. Like Hyde, she was deceptively youthful in her appearance.

With her short white hair that was often spiked straight up and brilliant greenish-yellow eyes, Ada frequently reminded Hyde of a birch tree in all its autumnal splendour. Her face was sweet and round, almost childlike. But anyone who spent time with her knew better.

There was an age to Ada. It settled around her like

a cloak. She'd seen the passage of time in the forests of Scotland.

Hyde locked the door and gathered the two packages. One was a scandalous romance between a dryad and a naiad, while the other was a reference on apple trees. "Off we go, then."

They took a moment to enjoy the stillness in the village. The scent of orange, cranberry, and spices lingered in the air. Lights flickered in the lamps, sending dancing shadows around them as they walked.

The faerie lights woven amidst the winter greenery decorated all the village shops. In the distance, Hyde heard the crackle and pop of the ritual fire in the park. There was a faint bubbling of cauldrons as well. All the signs of the beginnings of Yule festivities to come.

Hyde went past Roasted and Toasted, taking a left down the small lane leading into the fields behind the shops on Harbour Road. The path led to the beginnings of Ada's orchard. It wasn't a surprise to find the dryad already up and about with lanterns on the ground between the trees while she worked. "Morning."

"Hello." Ada waved at them, clambering down the

ladder. She pulled off her leather gloves, shoving them into her pocket. "What brings you out amongst my trees this early in the morning?"

"Books." Hyde lifted up the two packages to hold out to her. "Your romance."

"Hyde."

"Well, it is a romance novel. Don't be ashamed of your scandalous love of dryad and naiad trysts." Hyde failed to hide their grin when Ada grumbled at them. "Also, the apple book."

"The compendium on the history and cultivating of rare apple trees?"

"Yes, the apple book."

"You are being difficult this morning. Want some apple chai? I brewed some this morning." Ada clutched the books under one arm, bending down to grab one of her lanterns off the ground. "Come, come. The stove in the barn is burning nice and warm this morning. We'll have some tea, and you can tell me all about what I missed while I was dancing amongst the trees the past few nights."

Harvests worked differently in and around the village. No one quite knew how or why, but the growing season tended to last longer and yield more. Emrys had once told Hyde that Myrddin blessed the ground itself to care for the foundlings in its borders.

It was possible. Hyde knew the orchard and farms did better than those a few villages over. The fishing off the loch often yielded more as well.

The foundlings loved the land—and it seemed to return the sentiment.

"Tell me about your troubles, my lovely book person." Ada drew Hyde out of their thoughts about the land.

"Three members of the Snodgrass family came to the village. My uncle Magnus Snodgrass died. No idea how or why. There's a theory, but they haven't confirmed it. He was a pile of ash in front of my shop." Hyde was still not completely sure how to process any of it. "Pacheco took Emrys for questioning."

"Of course he did. Those two." Ada shook her head and muttered about stubborn old fools. She grabbed a pot off the stove and poured it into two hand-carved wooden mugs. "What do you think? It's my new obsession. I've tried creating apple chai out of every type I have in the orchard. Do you know how much I've drunk recently?"

"No."

"Many cups. I couldn't decide on one, so I had to try all of them. Immediately." Ada handed her one of the mugs. She sat on one of the tall stools in the barn.

"Magnus Snodgrass. Dead as ash. He was but no more than an ass."

"Ada."

"Sorry. There's a rhyme stuck in my head now." She sipped her chai. "Hmm. Not my favourite. I'll have to pick another apple for next time. Any reason they came to the village? Not exactly a haunt most Snodgrasses would enjoy."

"What Snodgrass do you know other than me?"

"You'd be surprised." Ada set her mug down. She grabbed the books from the table, stowing them in a basket. "Now, I've apples to process and other things to take care of. I've maybe another week before I begin preparing for winter. Take the mug. I've carved loads of them. Maybe walk down Druid Lane and see if Emrys has returned home."

"Ada?"

"There's a fell omen in the air. I hear things whistling on the wind through the trees. And I found a rotten apple."

"Ada. You own an orchard of all manner of fruit trees. You're a dryad. I'd wager you've found many a rotten apple." Hyde sighed. "Don't you have a bucket of rotten apples?"

"That was one time—and I was proving a point."

Ada humphed at them. "And you were sworn to secrecy."

"By you. It's not breaking the pact if I'm talking to you about it."

"You may be correct." Ada waved them out of the barn. "Go see if Emrys is home."

She grabbed the lantern, swinging it at her side and singing merrily. The tune was bright and cheerful, and the words were melancholy. She spoke of last loves and stubborn fools; Hyde wondered just how many secrets the mischievous and mysterious dryad held.

They sipped the chai, finding it sweet and spicy with a hint of tart apple. Druid Lane was on the other side of the village. They were halfway there when a crow landed on their shoulder, tapping them insistently on the side of the head.

"Am I being summoned, then?" Hyde reached up and gently stroked his inky feathers. "All right, then."

Walking across the lane, Hyde made their way to the post office. They opened the door, smiling at the chimes. Odin immediately flew over to his witch's shoulder.

"What sort of day is it, Hyde?" Morrigan asked.

"I'm a talkative they at the moment. Subject to

change." Hyde always enjoyed being around Morrigan. She exuded calm and collected, something they envied. "Everything all right? Odin was quite insistent on my coming over. Did I miss a delivery?"

"I cast my runes this morning as always." Morrigan searched behind the counter for several seconds. She tended to use her magic to amplify her other senses to aid her. "Ah. There they are. Promise me you'll be careful. There's a fell omen this midwinter."

"A fell omen?" Hyde wished if villagers were going to give ominous predictions, they would be more specific. A fell omen could be anything from accidentally burning a book to stubbing their toe. "Were you, by chance, in commune with Ada this morning?"

Morrigan lifted her head up from behind the counter. "No. Why?"

"She mentioned a fell omen."

"Not a felled tree?" Morrigan grinned. She stood back up and set a packet on the counter. "I made this for you."

Hyde picked it up, giving the velvet pouch a sniff. "Rosemary, sage, bay, and something earthy."

"The nose knows." Morrigan chuckled when Hyde sighed at her. "Never you mind about the something earthy. I've made you a protection bundle. Put it in your pocket for me."

Hyde tried to feel touched by the concern and not exasperated by the vaguely murky warning. "Thank you."

"Thank me by being careful."

To their amusement, Hyde found themselves waved off for a second time that morning. They stepped out into the early morning shadows. The little velvet packet in their pocket had a pleasant enough scent, but they did slightly feel like a roast dinner in the making.

After stopping at the bookshop to check on the cats, Hyde continued to Emrys's cottage. A merlin falcon flew from one of the trees to perch on their shoulder. They frowned when it bonked their head.

"Something wrong?" Hyde wasn't comforted by the distressed bird. It made them think something was definitely wrong with Emrys. "I'm going to check on him. What is it with things being in double this morning? Feathered fowl. Fell omens. Isn't it supposed to be things coming in threes?"

No lights were on inside Emrys's cottage. Hyde pulled the bell and then knocked with no response. They peered through the first window but didn't see any movement.

"He's not home."

Hyde nearly jumped out of their skin. "Wilfred. What the blazes? You almost gave me a heart attack."

"Not possible for a vampire. And I'd know since I'm your doctor. Also, not to repeat myself, you're a vampire. How did you not hear me?"

Hyde waved a hand as if to bat away the question. "Where's Emrys?"

"I'd hazard a guess that he's at the police station in Kyle of Lochalsh. That's where Pacheco usually questions witnesses—and suspects." Wilfred frowned at the falcon on their shoulder. "Don't bother the foundling. Emrys can handle himself."

The merlin falcon made a shrill, chattering noise, which made Hyde wince. It finally flew off. They winced at the slight pressure on their shoulder.

Wilfred waggled his finger at the bird now perched on a tree branch in front of the cottage. "Behave yourself. He'll be back soon enough."

"You really think he's in Kyle?"

"Hyde. You can't drive to the police station. It's far too early." Wilfred followed them when they began walking purposefully back towards Harbour Road. "For all his faults, Pacheco won't accuse someone without evidence."

Hyde scoffed loudly. They believed it to an extent,

but they'd also watched enough telly to know evidence could be manufactured by the real killer. "They're always narky at each other."

"Maybe. I think of it as two people who secretly like each other, poking to get a reaction."

"That's not a very healthy relationship. You shouldn't needle someone to the point of anger to show you like them." Hyde never understood how some non-autistic minds worked. They pushed it aside as unimportant to decipher at the moment. "And to answer your other question, I can drive—I prefer not to. If needs must, I can ride my bicycle."

"It's five in the morning."

"I can see fine." Hyde sometimes thought their sight was better in the dark than in the bright sunlight. "Don't you have a clinic to open?"

"Don't you have a shop to open?" Wilfred stubbornly followed them all the way to Between the Leaves. "Hyde, please be careful. Magnus wasn't murdered on your doorstep by accident."

"Not sure murders happen by accident. Wouldn't that defeat the purpose?" Hyde scrubbed their face with their hands for a moment. "I am being as cautious as vampirely possible."

With a sigh and a nod, Wilfred turned and headed off towards the village clinic.

Hyde had always seen Emrys as a father figure. He was the closest they'd had. The villagers were all their family. Aunts, uncles, cousins—all made up of those not related to them by blood.

And Hyde had no qualms about doing everything in their power to protect their *true* family.

10

TERESA

WAKING UP IN WINTER WAS ALWAYS TEN TIMES harder. Teresa enjoyed sunlight. She tried to appreciate each season and cycle, but the shorter days could be rough.

She dragged herself out of bed and thanked the goddess for another day. Her back cracked as she stretched. *Not enough tea in the world for a morning like this.*

The wind had picked up suddenly. It buffeted against the bus. She mentally thanked Emrys for magically reinforcing the windows after Aadil had replaced them when a storm the previous year had broken them.

By the time Teresa had showered and dressed for the day, someone was banging on the window. She

wasn't surprised to find Hyde. They were usually awake before her, given they didn't actually need sleep.

"Emrys hasn't come back to the village." Hyde continued rambling as Teresa pulled them onto the bus. "He's probably at the police station in Kyle."

"And you want to check on him?" Teresa wasn't surprised when Hyde nodded. "How about I whip us up a couple of breakfast tacos and some tea? We can prepare ourselves for assailing the police station."

"Maybe politely speaking. Not sure a full assault is required." Hyde frowned at her for a second. "Ah. Joking. Not literal."

"I mean, I'm not opposed." Teresa grabbed a few things out of the smaller of the two fridges. It was one she used for her personal food. The larger one was strictly for commercial purposes. The entire downstairs was mainly kitchen space. "Grab a couple of mugs for me?"

In no time at all, Teresa had fixed them up a quick breakfast. They noshed on the tacos while drinking tea. Hyde filled her in on their early-morning adventures.

"How about I take us on my motorcycle?" Teresa sipped her tea after inhaling the breakfast taco she'd thrown together. "Plenty of time for us to ride to Kyle of Lochalsh and return before either of us needs to open shop for the day."

"On your bike?"

"I have a helmet for you. Custom-made. It arrived last week, and I haven't had a chance to show you." Teresa darted up the stairs to retrieve the package. "Here."

Hyde carefully pulled out the motorcycle helmet. "It has bat wings on the front."

"Just so people know it's you."

Hyde snickered with Teresa. "It's brilliant."

Her vintage BMW motorcycle was one of her prized possessions. It was almost identical to one that had been ridden by the first witch to travel the world on a bike. As one of the women Teresa admired most, she'd chosen her preferred mode of transport because of her.

The ride to Kyle of Lochalsh took fifteen minutes at most. Teresa enjoyed every second of having Hyde's arms tightly wrapped around her. If they hadn't been worried about Emrys, it would've been hard not to find an excuse to prolong the journey.

For Teresa, her motorcycle had been the first step in making decisions for herself. She'd thrown off the weight of family expectations. It had been a choice she'd made for herself.

A few minutes from Kyle, Hyde finally relaxed into the ride. They'd been tense for much of it. She wondered if maybe now she'd be able to convince the vampire to go on a bike holiday; it might be asking too much.

As Teresa approached the police station, she spotted Emrys standing outside. Hyde practically launched themselves off the motorcycle. They struggled for a few seconds before finally getting the helmet off their head.

"Foundling. Everything all right?" Emrys caught on quickly to how concerned Hyde had been. "I'm fine. Not a scratch on me. He didn't put me on the rack. No other odious forms of torture were involved. Just a few questions."

"It's five in the morning." Hyde glanced back at Teresa, who held up six fingers. "Six in the morning, probably closer to seven at this point. I worried."

Emrys patted them on the arm. He inspected the helmet they were holding. "Nice bat wings."

"Aren't they?" Hyde showed them off, seeming even more pleased when Pacheco audibly groaned. "You aren't being arrested?"

"I never intended to arrest Emrys. I believe he is fully capable of committing murder in defence of a foundling. He'd never do it in front of your shop, though." Pacheco made what Teresa considered to be an excellent point. "The only reason to make it happen there would be to point the finger at you."

"I didn't murder Magnus."

"I'm aware. You're the least violent and blood-thirsty vampire I've ever known." Pacheco ran his hand tiredly across his face. He seemed absolutely exhausted to Teresa. "Your aunt intends to have a brief ceremony here in the Highlands before returning home."

"Okay." Hyde wrapped their arms around the helmet. They glanced back at Teresa. "Am I supposed to care more about his death?"

There was a lost tone to their voice that tugged at her heartstrings. Teresa went to answer, but Pacheco beat her to it. He spoke before either she or Emrys could.

"They broke the familial bond. Not you. I'd say it's normal to be conflicted over his death. Normal to not feel the loss deeply. Don't judge yourself harshly for it." Pacheco nodded to Emrys, who stood beside him. "I made mistakes when you came to South Myrddin. And I am profoundly sorry for not intervening sooner. You don't owe anyone your grief, Hyde. Not even those who share your surname."

The vampire elder spun on his heel and disappeared into the police station, leaving them staring after him stunned. Teresa went over to Hyde, slipping her arm around their shoulders. It was easy to see they had no idea how to quantify the change in Pacheco.

"You're seeing the vampire I fell in love with aeons ago. He's not so bad when he doesn't have a massive stake up his...." Emrys trailed off when Teresa cleared her throat. "How about we head back to the village? Does anyone fancy breakfast? I'm starving. I'll tell you all about the little bits of information I've gleaned about the case while I've been stuck here."

"Should you do that?" Teresa couldn't help asking despite her curiosity to know more.

"He never said I couldn't. I'll take that as permission and pretend to ask for forgiveness later." Emrys smiled mischievously at them. He pulled his pipe out of his pocket and lit it. "I'll see you in the village at Roasted and Toasted. I could use some calming tea to fortify myself."

"Hyde."

They all turned towards the police station when Phineas called out to them. Teresa kept a close eye on him, not trusting any of Hyde's family. No matter how harmless he appeared, they all seemed to be snakes in the grass.

"I was hoping we could speak." Phineas started forwards, only to stop when Emrys moved up to stand beside Hyde. He shoved his hands into his pockets, shifting uneasily on his feet. "I mean no harm."

"The Snodgrasses have done plenty of harm." Emrys puffed on his pipe. "What makes you different?"

"I... I...." Phineas stared down at the pavement for a few moments. "I didn't know what Father had planned."

11

HYDE

For several long seconds, Hyde watched their cousin suspiciously. People often talked about body language. They'd watched an entire documentary about it with Bram the other night while he gave incredibly colourful commentary.

They tried to analyse Phineas's posture. *What am I even looking for? He's standing. What the dickens am I supposed to decipher?*

He stands like everyone... like a vampire.

He vaguely resembles a tree or a building or anything else that is just standing there.

"Hyde?" Teresa leaned in closer to whisper to them. "Hyde. You've been staring in silence for about a full three minutes. We've gone past awkward into concerned. Are you all right?"

Hyde blinked a few times before turning towards her. "I was trying to figure out what his body language means."

"Ah. Right. And?" Teresa stopped whispering since Hyde hadn't bothered. They didn't understand the point since Phineas had vampiric hearing like themselves. "Discover anything?"

"I think he's standing." Hyde sighed when Teresa snorted in obvious amusement. "What am I supposed to look for? He's just... standing."

"He can also hear you perfectly fine." Emrys tapped his pipe on his arm a few times before popping one end into his mouth and lighting it with a snap of his fingers. "I concur with your assessment. He is, in fact, standing."

"Can we all stop saying standing? It doesn't even sound like a word." Teresa giggled a little hysterically.

"Right." Hyde attempted to refocus their mind on something other than body language. "Why did you come here?"

"Father said he wanted to—"

"No. Not Eunice and Magnus. Your father, I understand. He wanted the grimoire—and me gone. Why did you come? You could've said no easily." Hyde had been isolated as a young vampire before being thrust out of the family. They had spent some time with their cousin but not much, not enough to figure him out. "Why come with them?"

"Our family likes to keep secrets—even from one another. I was hoping to figure out what Father was doing." Phineas shoved his hands into his pockets, shifting from one foot to the other. He cleared his throat loudly. "I have no idea why Mother came. They certainly weren't known for travelling together. Our family is odd that way, isn't it?"

Hyde glanced from Phineas to Emrys, who offered what they believed was a comforting smile. "Not my family. Not after they threw me away like a bag of rubbish."

"I imagine your father was far too *detached* to physically throw you out. He'd have someone else do it." Phineas wasn't wrong. "He does so very much believe in delegating things, even if it's to his younger brother or other members of the family."

"You're not wrong. Cassian Snodgrass never liked to get his own hands dirty." Hyde was suddenly utterly exhausted. Family history always made them weary. They couldn't remember the last time they spoke about their father. "I want tea. And my cats."

"Right." Emrys held his pipe in one hand and reached out to grasp Phineas's shoulder with his other. "How about you and I have a chat while those two head back to the village?"

To avoid further conversation, Hyde pushed the helmet back onto their head. They tuned everything out, returning to where Teresa had parked her motorcycle. They wished, not for the first time, for the ability some vampires had to disappear into the shadows.

That had never been one of their talents.

The journey back to the village was far less exhilarating and enjoyable. Hyde settled into the numbing silence in their mind. No thoughts. No words. They closed their eyes and tried to keep a tight grip on Teresa until they reached South Myrddin.

"Go on. I'll be on the bus if you need me." Teresa nudged them towards the bookshop.

The hum of their shop was almost immediately calming. Their frayed nerves settled with the gentle, magical massage. Mortar and Pestle joined them by the counter.

Village magic was woven into the lights, books, and shelves. Not Hyde's—they didn't have magic—but from the other villagers. Decades of love and acceptance had sunk into the walls themselves.

Hyde breathed easily for the first time in ages.

They'd been unsettled since the Snodgrasses appeared but unable to put it into words.

Mortar leapt up onto the counter. "Were you enjoying the quiet?"

With a dignified meow, Mortar rubbed her head against Hyde's hand.

A chime drew their attention to the door. They groaned when Eunice swanned inside, appearing as if she owned everything around her. The beginnings of a better mood vanished instantly.

"This is where you spend your life?" Eunice inspected the shelf closest to the counter, picking up one of the books. "In this shop?"

Hyde fluffed up indignantly, much like their cats. "Between the Leaves is the most wonderful treasure that has ever been gifted to me."

More than you or anyone else in the family ever gave me.

"My apologies."

Hyde didn't know what she was apologising for— or if they cared what the reason was. "Were you looking for a book?"

"I hoped to reconnect with you. We haven't had time to chat, what with everything happening."

Everything happening?

Despite not always grasping tone or context, Hyde

thought the air of casualness odd. They rested a hand on Mortar's head, allowing the engine-like purr to calm them. Nothing could happen to them in their shop.

Their castle.

Their home.

Hyde wished they had a better grasp of body language. They had no idea if Eunice was being sincere despite the oddness of her comment. "By 'everything,' do you mean Magnus trying to murder me and then being killed himself?"

Pestle inserted himself into the conversation. He joined Mortar on the counter. Both cats stared at Eunice, who didn't seem to fully realise the danger their chaos kittens could pose. She smiled at the two of them.

"It's obvious *you* didn't kill him, so I don't believe anything prevents us from having a cordial conversation." Eunice spoke with the same mild, cultured tone as most of the Snodgrasses. Cold to the point that Hyde expected icicles to drip from her tongue. "You've done well for yourself."

"I have." Hyde had always wondered if their family purposefully sought out people of a similar nature or if it was learned behaviour. "I'm content."

"One should strive for the best."

"Should *one*?" Hyde mimicked her tone unconsciously. They shook their head with a grimace, almost tempted to wipe their tongue to rid themselves of the sensation. "Why was Uncle Magnus here? I know it wasn't to apologise to me."

"The journal, darling. The journal. Who sent it to you?" Eunice continued inspecting the slightly crooked bookshelf. Her cold blue eyes darted briefly towards Hyde. "Was there a note?"

For a moment, Hyde almost wanted to cackle wildly. The burst of almost macabre amusement bubbled up inside them. The artifice had shed from Eunice. It had always been about the family grimoire.

The Snodgrass journal held secrets, tales, and all manner of important information jotted down by members of the family going back centuries. Someone had sent it to Hyde months earlier. They'd never been able to figure out who or even why.

Most families had a grimoire, whether it was a vampire, witch, or other magical being. Theirs was the Snodgrass journal. They were closely guarded—passed down from one generation to the next. A wealth of knowledge was held between magically strengthened, leather-bound pages.

"Answer me."

The sudden harsh demand in Eunice's voice made

Hyde look at her. Nothing had changed aside from a sudden fire in those cold blue eyes. Her porcelain skin remained perfect. Her snow-white short hair sculpted perfectly around her face to frame her strong jaw and almost hawklike gaze.

"I have no idea," Hyde answered truthfully. They had no intentions of being intimidated by any of the Snodgrasses.

The door slammed open before Eunice could pester them again. Phineas rushed inside, tripping over the carpet. He stammered an apology, then froze when he spotted Eunice at the counter.

"Mother." Phineas frowned at his mother. His gaze flitted from Eunice back to Hyde. "Why are you here?"

"Reconnecting with my niece."

The lie dripped from Eunice's tongue far easier than it would've Hyde's. They rolled their eyes. Mortar and Pestle sensed the growing tension and sat up, paying closer attention to the energy in the room.

"Leave her alone, Mother." Phineas moved closer to Eunice. He ran his fingers through his wavy ginger hair. "Why don't I take you home? There's no point in remaining in South Myrddin. You hate the Highlands."

"Hate is a strong word. And no, I have questions. I

want answers." Eunice glowered at him when he went to take her arm. "I'm not finished here."

Mortar had apparently had enough of them. She jumped off the counter towards them, causing Eunice to move out of the way. Both cats hissed at them, stalking menacingly towards them and herding them to the door.

"Have a good day." Hyde waved merrily, content to allow their cats to handle the situation. They wandered over to the tea station to find the tin of treats. "Such good furry menaces, aren't you?"

The door shut behind the mother and son. Phineas had somehow managed to convince Eunice to leave. Hyde had no doubts it wasn't the last they'd hear from her.

It always came back to the grimoire.

Always.

12

"Leave them alone, Mother."

The noise caught her attention. Teresa was prepping for opening the taco bus for the day. She gave the rice one last stir, then leaned across the counter to get a better view out the window.

Eunice Snodgrass stood in front of the bookshop, glowering coldly at her son. "I want answers. He came for the grimoire. Why? Who sent it to them? What drew Magnus here only to be murdered?"

"Hyde wouldn't kill him."

"I'm sure." Eunice sneered at him. "They might know who did. The druid, maybe."

"We should go home."

"You were the one who wanted to come with us. Insisted on it." She narrowed her eyes. "Why?"

"Mother. We're supposed to collect Father's ashes from the police. Perhaps we should do that now?" Phineas went from practically a cooked noodle to a solid rock. He grasped her by the elbow and began guiding her down the pavement towards a parked vehicle. "Quit drawing attention to us. You won't get your answers this way."

Teresa watched the two until they'd driven off. *How very, very curious.*

Crouching down to sift through the storage cabinets built underneath the counters, Teresa hunted for the serving containers. They were specially made for her, designed to fit three tacos with space for salsas and other sauces.

She found a new box of the containers hidden behind a bag of rice. "Aha! There you are."

The weekly menu included a slow-roasted pork mole along with the usual blood sausage one. Queenie, the local butcher, had brought her a beautiful pork shoulder. One of the best things about running a taco bus in South Myrddin was having easy access to products from the nearby farms.

The lunch rush made the early afternoon fly by. Teresa barely had a moment to take a breath. Things calmed down by three, as it usually did. She'd run out of just about everything she'd prepped, leaving just enough to whip up a small snack for herself.

A loud yowl pierced the air while Teresa was washing the dishes. She spun around and caught sight of DCI Pacheco walking Hyde away from the bookshop. He guided them into a vehicle and drove off before she could get out of the bus.

Teresa jogged into the street, only for the vehicle to already be out of sight. "What the…?"

Anger surged through her. Teresa rushed back to the bookshop, checking on Mortar and Pestle. She made sure they had food and water, then locked up both Between the Leaves and Guac-A-Mole.

Pushing past the simmering rage and panic, Teresa tried to think clearly. She caught sight of Bram and Emrys in a heated debate down the street towards the park. They provided her with a suitable target for her anger.

Teresa stalked down the pavement until she caught up to them. "While you're busy being spiky with each other, Pacheco just drove off with Hyde."

"What?" Emrys twisted away from Bram, seeming to immediately tune him out. "Why?"

"How should I know? I didn't even get a chance to ask a single thing. It has to be about Magnus's murder. Why else?" Teresa rubbed her hand over her chest when her breathing began to pick up. "Is he arresting them? What if he's arresting them? He can't."

"Jonatan is a fool, but he's not *that* foolish." Emrys ignored the snort from Bram, who seemed to know something Teresa didn't. "I'll go check on them."

Before Teresa or Bram could say anything, Emrys had stalked off. He was gone faster than some vampires she'd seen vanish in smoke. It almost made her pity Pacheco if he *had* actually arrested Hyde.

"Should we…?" Teresa trailed off, unsure of how to complete her sentence. She nodded towards where Emrys had stood. "Go after him? Or stay here?"

"Stay here and miss the druid-vampire romantic fireworks? Never." Bram smirked ferally. "Fancy a jaunt on the fae side?"

Teresa narrowed her eyes. "What? Being one with moss and possessed rocks—in your case, at least?"

"Emrys isn't the only one capable of slipping through a ley line to travel." Bram held a hand out to her. "It shouldn't be too unpleasant for you."

"You're not filling me with confidence." She eyed his hand with a justifiable sense of trepidation. "Slipping through a ley line?"

"Surfing. Coasting. Travelling. Skipping." Bram waved his arm around dramatically before dropping into a graceful bow. He peered up at her with a mad twinkle in his eyes. "Waltz with me through the ley?"

Teresa sighed. She didn't know Bram like Hyde did, but he certainly seemed to fit the description of a semi-feral bard to a T. "Comport?"

"Oh. Good word. You like to play. I knew Hyde wouldn't pick a fading flower." Bram stood back up. He shoved his wild brown hair into some semblance of control. "In all seriousness, it's quicker than a flash. You might have the briefest moment of oddness."

"Oddn—" Teresa stretched her hand out to take his and immediately found herself yanked off her feet.

It was as if the world were suddenly nothing but wisps of shadow and magic. Oddness described the sensation accurately. She felt like her entire being had dived into a fast-flowing river of pure, raw magic. They popped out a short distance from the police station.

Teresa shook her head a few times, attempting to clear her vision. "I feel like I ate a batch of those mushrooms Queenie always mutters about."

"Sheep shifters know all about grazing the wrong

things." Bram strode forwards. His long legs carried him quickly; Teresa was by no means short, but she had to jog to catch up to him. "Emrys is already inside. I can't let him have all the fun."

"Fun?"

Aside from the trip on the ley side, none of this felt like fun to Teresa. Her anxiety was spiking. She pushed it to the side, focusing instead on getting to Hyde.

"A druid, witch, and fae walk into a police station." Bram didn't finish his joke. Emrys and Pacheco both glared at him, although he seemed utterly unfazed by it. "Where is the poppet?"

"In there." Emrys nodded towards what was clearly an interrogation room.

"Why are they in there?" Teresa asked.

The question went unanswered as Emrys and Bram jumped in with queries of their own. They talked over themselves, and Pacheco attempted unsuccessfully to respond. Teresa was half tempted to cover her ears like Hyde sometimes did.

"They're not under arrest," Pacheco shouted over the din outside the interrogation room. "I'm not even questioning them."

Silence reigned for all of a second. Teresa turned

her head when the door opened. She smiled when Hyde appeared.

Hyde poked their head out of the room, pulling their headphones off. "Have I missed something?"

"We thought he arrested you." Teresa gestured towards Pacheco. "Did he?"

"No." Hyde's gaze darted between the crowded group in the hallway. An awkward silence settled for a prolonged moment. "We had blood chai with biscuits."

"Very civilised," Teresa whispered with a grin. "Why *are* you here?"

They paused for another moment, as if trying to find the right words. "Family oddness."

"So, the usual?" Teresa was relieved when Hyde snickered. "What brand of odd?"

"The matriarch of the Snodgrass coven left a secret last will and testament. Though...." Hyde frowned at Pacheco. "How could it be a secret if everyone knew about it? That doesn't make sense. Anyway, whatever, she named me her successor."

"She did what now?" Teresa had honestly thought the majority, if not all, of the Snodgrasses would prefer to think Hyde didn't exist. "Did she send the grimoire?"

"No idea." Hyde pulled their cap off and dragged their fingers roughly through their ginger curls. "She had what her doctor claimed was a genetic blood disorder. She couldn't ingest any form of sustenance. Maybe it gave her a conscience? I don't want it—any of it. What the dickens would I do with control of a coven that loathes my entire existence?"

"It might explain Magnus's sudden interest in tracking you down," Pacheco interjected.

"Sudden desire to murder me. He wouldn't have wanted anyone else to have control over the coven or me." Hyde took a step closer to Teresa. They leaned into her with a tired sigh. "It doesn't explain who'd want to kill him. I had no idea about her estate."

"No one thinks you killed him." Pacheco spoke blandly, as if he were repeating himself for the hundredth time. "No one. I wanted you to be aware of the will. I just found out."

"How?" Emrys had suddenly become very attentive to the conversation. "Wouldn't you have known already?"

"When I say secret, it was kept quiet. No one knew. Someone delivered it anonymously to me last night." Pacheco held a hand up when Emrys and Bram immediately went to speak. "I'm aware of how suspicious that is. My purpose in bringing

Hyde to the station was to make them aware and cautious."

"If someone killed Magnus for control, they might be after Hyde." Teresa slipped her arm protectively around them. "Who knew about the will?"

"I've questioned several members of the family. No one will admit to knowing about it. Eunice and Phineas are coming in to speak with me for a second time. My inquiry continues." Pacheco's gaze drifted over to Emrys. "Everyone should be careful."

"By everyone, he means me," Hyde muttered. "Can I go home now? Books won't sell themselves."

"Pretty sure Mortar and Pestle could sell the books." Teresa led Hyde out of the police station after Pacheco nodded. "Who in your family would want control the most?"

"Every single one of them?" Hyde shrugged. They blinked in the rare bit of bright winter sun. "I wasn't exaggerating when I said they were a pit of vipers. I always thought Phineas was an exception, but maybe he isn't."

"Why don't we make our way back to the village? We can chat over some tea and biscuits. Very civilised." Bram held out both hands. "I can carry both of you."

"I don't fancy a trip through fields of energy."

Hyde stared suspiciously at his hand. They glanced over at Teresa with hope in their eyes. "Motorcycle? Broom? Anything?"

"When have you ever seen a witch on a broom? That's as cliché as vampires and garlic." Teresa patted their shoulder comfortingly.

"Garlic is delicious in a blood tomato sauce on pizza." Hyde leaned into Teresa's touch. "How about a walk?"

"To the village?"

"It's probably about an hour and a half, maybe closer to two." Hyde sidestepped Bram, who still had his hand out. "I can't do surfing the ley today. Makes my head fuzzy. Last time, I had nightmares for days."

"You are a vampire. You don't require sleep." Pacheco rubbed his forehead, seeming suddenly very tired.

"I nap," Hyde insisted grumpily. "Just because you never indulge in life's pleasures."

"Napping?"

Hyde turned away from Pacheco and back towards Teresa. "Walk with me?"

"I'd love to." Teresa slipped her hand into Hyde's. They headed away from the three others, moving towards the walking path leading out of Kyle of

Lochalsh. It wound through the Highlands to South Myrddin. "You okay?"

Hyde managed a somewhat believable smile. "I don't understand any of this. I don't... I just don't understand. It's illogical."

"We both know people who consider themselves normal can be the most illogical of all."

13

HYDE

The air was crisp and damp. Hyde thought they might be in for an early snow this winter. They could smell it on the wind.

Their brief glimpse of the winter sun had vanished behind a blanket of fluffy dark clouds. It suited the landscape around them. Shades of brown, barren trees, and the darkest pops of colour from evergreens. There was a beauty to the harsh edges of this time of year.

"This feels quite storybook-esque." Teresa climbed over a style, waiting for Hyde to follow. They clambered through a dense thicket out into open fields with a narrow path through it. "No breadcrumbs to be found."

"I'm not sure these are a Hansel and Gretel sort of

woods. Also, they were absolute pricks. They ate her house." Hyde snickered when Teresa flicked a twig at them. "Not sure I like this start to midwinter. It's usually such a joyous time of year."

"There's some joy. Aren't you the new head of the Snodgrass family? Or matriarch? Theytriarch?"

"Theytriarch is not a word," Hyde grumbled. They kicked at a pebble, launching it a ways down the path. "I don't want it. The grimoire is interesting. I couldn't give a fig about the rest of it."

"Hyde."

"They don't get to come into my life now. I found my family here in South Myrddin. They're a poison. Venom. They ruin everything. They want me to surrender power—and they can have it." Hyde bent down to grab a stray twig, crushing it to powder in their hand. "Boundaries are good. I read that."

"They are." Teresa took their hand, gently unclenching their fingers and brushing away the dust. "They don't deserve you. Tell them all to sod off. Or have Bram do it. It'll be lyrical and biting."

"It would be something." Hyde glanced over at Teresa for a moment. They went for a completely unsubtle change of conversation. The bog of family mess could wait for another day or century as far as they were concerned. "You could've let him take you back through the ley."

"I could. But I'd rather walk with you. You know, I read *Vampires 101: Things To Know When Dating One*, and it doesn't mention anything about a fear of ley lines." Teresa snickered when Hyde shoved her playfully. "It does state, and I quote, 'one should be careful of what scents one wears so as not to annoy the sensitive nostrils of their vampire lover.'"

"It does not."

"It does." Teresa skipped ahead when Hyde lunged for her. "There's an entire section on how to handle long nights when your vampire is awake and how to help care for their teeth."

"I take perfect care of my teeth. I'm beginning to think a werewolf wrote that book." Hyde caught up to Teresa. They felt lighter than they had in days—since Magnus and his entourage showed up. Was it wrong to smile and be happy after a murder? They pushed the question from their mind, not wanting to feel overwhelming confusion. "Who was the author?"

"You're not writing a letter to the author telling them how wrong they are." Teresa snickered when Hyde grumbled under their breath. "You could also create your own how-to guide."

Despite the clouds overhead and the crisp air, it

was a beautiful day of the gloomy, cosy, almost winter variety. Hyde ran their fingers along a barren bush. The few remaining leaves clung to the tops, dry and fragile like old parchment. They had a feeling it was going to be a cold winter.

"What was your grandmother like?"

Hyde considered the question while they ambled underneath a windswept tree that looked like it were crawling over a rocky hill, limbs outstretched towards the sky. "Terrifying."

"That's... somewhat descriptive."

"Mildred Snodgrass ground everyone under her heel. She bowed to no one. Ice in her veins. All the clichés to describe an intimidating vampire with centuries of life behind her." Hyde paused to inspect the stone boundary around one of the large farms in the area before climbing over the style. "From what Pacheco said, she'd been content for the past decade or so to allow my father, Cassian, and my uncle Magnus to jostle for control. When she became ill, she wrote a last will and testament in secret, supposedly. It was sent anonymously to him. And there's no way to know for sure if she sent me the grimoire—or why she did any of it."

They meandered through the fields in silence for a while. Hyde allowed the sounds of the Highlands to wash over them. Their hand was firmly held in Teresa's. It was soothing to let the crisp breeze, birdsong, and whistling wind buffet them from the confusion plaguing their mind.

The path led them from one farm to the next before they finally arrived at the outskirts of South Myrddin. Hyde was surprised to see Phineas sitting on a stone boundary, staring across the field of a farm for sale. They hadn't expected him to be *out* in nature.

"Phineas," Hyde called out to him when they got closer, seeing no way to sneak around him. They tightened their hand on Teresa's. "What are you doing here?"

"Hyde." Phineas hopped off the stone wall. He dropped the branch in his hand; he seemed embarrassed to have been caught. They didn't quite understand why. His gaze shifted over to Teresa. "Hyde's person."

Teresa nodded at him. "Hyde's cousin."

They narrowed their gaze at him when he hadn't answered their question. "Did you know about the will? About the grimoire being sent to me?"

"No?" Phineas cleared his throat loudly. He scratched his head before coughing a few times. "No."

"Right." Hyde might not have mastered figuring

out emotions, tone, or motive, but even they saw through the obvious lie. "Phineas?"

"Must be running. I hear Mother calling me." Phineas tripped over the branch he'd dropped, collected himself, and then vanished rapidly.

"I'm probably not the best person to throw stones, but... that was odd." Hyde had only a few memories of their cousin. He'd been less standoffish yet more quirky than the rest of the family. "Why was he here?"

"Enjoying a bit of nature? Avoiding his mother?" Teresa crouched down to pick up the branch he'd dropped. She frowned at it, lifting it up to get a closer look. "What's this?"

Hyde leaned in to see the dried leaves tangled with the branch. It had been hidden underneath it. They were definitely not from the same plant or tree. "Phyllan pyr. I saw a sketch of it in the family grimoire—I looked it up after Pacheco mentioned it."

"We should call Fynn." Teresa tried not to dislodge the dried leaves while they inspected it. "And don't touch it."

"It's deadly for vampires when ingested. I'm hardly going to have a nibble on a plant that can kill me." Hyde rolled their eyes. "I've never once had the urge to nosh on a dry leaf, particularly one with murderous intentions."

"Why does Phineas have it in the first place?" Teresa held the branch gingerly in her hand as if she expected it to implode or latch on to Hyde. "Why the... what was he doing out here with this?"

With a shrug, Hyde focused on their phone and messaging DI Baines. They trusted Fynn not to get narky about their finding evidence. He responded immediately, telling them to stay put.

Strangely, it was not the first time they'd found evidence while on a walk. The past few months had been... odd. They hoped things calmed down sooner rather than later.

Hyde moved closer to inspect the phyllan pyr. "You...."

"No licking the evidence."

"One time. I did it one time—and it wasn't deadly to vampires." Hyde used their phone to take a few photos of both the dried leaves and the branch. "Maybe he didn't realise he dropped it?"

"Maybe."

The phyllan pyr brought far more questions than answers. Had Phineas been involved in the death of his father? Why else would he be casually carrying around what was likely the murder weapon?

"Does a dried bit of plant count as a weapon?"

"A method of murder if nothing else." Teresa purposefully kept it away from Hyde. "Phineas definitely wasn't my first choice for who might've done it."

"I want to ask him why."

"Hyde."

"I have to go talk to him. Wait for Fynn." Hyde darted forwards to give Teresa a hug, then took off as fast as they could go.

I have to know why.

14

"Hyde. Bollocks." Teresa had no chance of catching up to a vampire at full speed.

Panic fired through her like fireworks in her veins. She mentally flailed, trying to figure out what to do. If Phineas was the killer, she didn't want Hyde to confront him alone, but she couldn't leave until Fynn arrived.

Fight or flight?

Why doesn't anyone ever talk about freezing when my brain is so sodding overwhelmed it does nothing but flail like a newborn giraffe trying to walk?

She had no doubt Hyde had hyper-focused on all the unanswered questions, gotten fixated on Phineas, and taken off without stopping to think. It wasn't a

surprise. She still had to somehow drag herself out of the abyss of anxiety.

Teresa carefully set the evidence on top of the stone wall behind her. She took out her phone and called Fynn. "Pick up. Pick up."

"I'm almost the—"

"Hyde took off to ask Phineas questions about the murder," Teresa interrupted him.

"Of course they did. Text Emrys, will you? I'll call the chief inspector. Do you have a bag or something you can put the leaves into? Bring it with you to the village, and I'll head straight there." Fynn disconnected the call without even saying goodbye.

Teresa glowered at her phone for a moment before putting it away. She searched in her backpack before finally finding an empty paper sack left over from a picnic lunch she'd had with Hyde the other day. The dried leaves fit in perfectly; she rolled the bag shut and took a few slow breaths. "Ah. I love the swing of panicked adrenaline and the rush of exhaustion when it falls away."

The walk to the village seemed to take longer on her own. Teresa hadn't heard anything from Fynn or anyone else. Her anxiety built with each step.

A cawing raven caught her attention. Teresa hesitated. A large group of blackbirds was in a tree off to her right. The hair on the back of her neck stood up.

The familiar warning prickled along her skin. She thought about how her Nan Brigid had taught her how to harness the magic within her. It was, in her words, an internal warning system. Or it was when her anxiety didn't drown it out.

Teresa reached into her pocket to grasp the amulet there. *Let's hope the murder of cawing crows isn't an ominous sign.*

The amulet was one she'd made after their last brush with murder. She'd created one for herself and for Hyde. A small measure of protection, one she'd found within her abuela's grimoire.

Picking up her pace, Teresa wished she had Hyde's speed or Bram's ability to travel ley lines. She was at least ten minutes or more from the village. She grabbed her phone, sending a text message to Fynn.

As a seer, Fynn wouldn't laugh off her sudden overwhelming sense of dread. He responded within seconds and told her someone was coming to meet her. She gripped her phone tightly and continued walking, hoping to meet them halfway.

Teresa pushed through a gap in the stone wall and into one of the outer pastures of Fraser's farm. She could see the village in the distance. *Finally.*

Another call from the crows drew her attention. Teresa didn't think they were being friendly. They were trying to warn her of something.

Muttering under her breath in a mix of Spanish, Latin, and Irish, Teresa weaved her magic around herself. She didn't have the aggressive or perhaps physically intimidating abilities of some. But she wasn't helpless either.

"Ah. The witch."

Teresa shivered at the icy tone of those two words. She twisted around to see Eunice had appeared in the gap in the wall. "Ah. A vampire."

"You don't deserve a Snodgrass." Eunice sneered at her.

"And the Snodgrasses never deserved Hyde." Teresa had no real defence against a vampire, particularly one of Eunice's age and power. "Why are you out here? If you're looking for your son, he's already taken off."

"Phineas?"

"He was sitting on the wall not ten minutes or so ago." Teresa decided not to mention the dried leaves they'd found. "Being one with nature doesn't seem like your thing, so why are you here?"

"Don't presume to know me. Phineas was late. I

thought he might be out here, and then I decided to enjoy a walk."

"Your outfit cost more than my bus. Nature *isn't* your thing." Teresa had learned from experience that keeping someone talking was critical to staying alive. She had nothing concrete, but her instincts told her Eunice had been involved with Magnus's death. "Why were you looking for Phineas? Shouldn't you know where your son is?"

"He's... such a disappointment."

"Phineas?"

"We had such hopes. Our son might be the Snodgrass leader one day—maybe even usurp Pacheco's role as vampire coven leader for the region eventually. But he's more like Hyde. Odd. Detached from what his role in the family is supposed to be." Eunice sighed dramatically. She made it sound like being different was the worst thing in the world. "We wasted so much effort on him."

Wasted?

What a—

Focus on not dying, not bad parenting.

"You never deserved Hyde." Teresa read between the lines while trying to inch backwards, putting distance between them. "Phineas didn't seem to know why you travelled with Magnus. He found it strange."

C'mon, you snotty vampire twit. Take the bait. Monologue like all villains wind up doing.

"No vision at all. He never sees beyond his alchemy." Eunice sighed once again.

Teresa was growing really tired of the belaboured yet elegant groans. "Alchemy?"

"He plays with wine." She made it sound small, yet Teresa wanted to know more.

"Nothing wrong with wine."

"He would've been the perfect puppet on the metaphorical throne." Eunice casually flicked a stray bit of fluff off her tailored jacket.

"Unlike Magnus?"

"Magnus, like the rest of his blood, had a fatal flaw. They never cede control to anyone outside the family line. I admired Mildred Snodgrass. She clutched power in her frail fist and refused to release it." Eunice adjusted her jacket sleeves, making herself the picture of perfection again. "It wouldn't normally come to me. I married into the family."

"But if Magnus, Hyde, and Phineas are out of the picture?"

"Oh, you are a clever witch. There are so many offshoots of the family due to its insular nature. All I require is the briefest gap to slip into." Eunice shrugged delicately. "Apathy sets in after a while. None of the next generation are ruthless or strong enough to oppose me."

Teresa shook her head. "What's the point? All you'd have is the grimoire. Pacheco still leads the vampire covens. Individual family ones don't have enough power to make a trail of dead bodies worth it."

"Ah, but the grimoire holds enough knowledge to wrest control from him." Eunice's gaze narrowed on her. "No one is going to stop me."

Power, and probably money, had always been quite a motive for murder. Teresa had no doubt at all who'd been behind Magnus's death. Eunice had seen the opportunity and leapt at it.

I need to get away from her.

The crows were a raucous cacophony above her. One dived down towards Eunice. The vampire shirked, dodging away from the feathered missile.

Even with their assistance, Teresa didn't stand a chance at outrunning the vampire. She had no intentions of giving up. At the very least, the crows would be a distraction.

Teresa bolted in the opposite direction of Eunice. She barely made it a few steps when a hand grabbed the back of her jacket. Icy fingers grazed her neck before she was yanked onto the ground. *Shite.*

Scrambling backwards, Teresa narrowly missed Eunice, who'd leapt at her. The vampire took a step towards her. There were scratches all over her face from the crow's assault.

"Rude of you to leave without even a goodbye. It's almost as if you're afraid of me." Eunice loomed over Teresa.

Well, bollocks.

15

HYDE

In their rush to catch up with Phineas, Hyde hadn't stopped to think about anything else. They shouldn't have left Teresa. Their brain had refused to let go of the confusion around their cousin and become hyper-focused.

It was surprisingly easy to find him. Phineas sat on a bench not far from the bookshop, making notes in a leather-bound journal. He looked up when Hyde skidded to a halt in front of him.

"Cousin."

"Did you kill your dad?" Hyde blurted out.

"I did not. Though I think my mother tried to frame me for it. The family crest should've had a scorpion instead of the silly bird on it for their propensity

to eat their young." Phineas laughed, his voice going a little shrill. "They wanted to mould me into the perfect vampire to carry on the next generation of Snodgrasses. I wasn't interested. And they didn't deserve the family secrets."

"You sent me the grimoire." Hyde stared at him, trying to put all the puzzle pieces together. "Why?"

"Grandmother changed towards the end. She worried the coven had stagnated. It needed change." He fidgeted with the cuff of one sleeve, buttoning and unbuttoning it. "I didn't want it. I never imagined Father would track it to you."

"How do you know Eunice was trying to frame you?" Hyde asked, referring to what he'd said earlier.

"The phyllan pyr was in Mother's study. She had several jars in an alcove hidden behind a bookshelf." Phineas dropped his gaze down to the floor. His fingers returned to worrying at the button. "I found it in my bag this morning."

"Phineas."

"I'm terrified she's killed Father and has decided to get rid of me at the same time. She'll go after you next. She wants power." Phineas jolted in surprise when Pacheco appeared behind them. Their cousin turned immediately toward the elder vampire. "You have to protect Hyde."

"What's going on?" Pacheco placed a hand on Phineas's shoulder.

"Wait. Hyde? Where's your witch person?" Phineas glanced in one direction, then the other, as though expecting Teresa to appear in front of them. "Weren't you together earlier?"

Hyde ignored both of them and grabbed their phone. They tried calling Teresa. "She's not answering. She always does when it's me."

"Eunice killed Magnus. She'll be after me and Hyde next," Phineas interjected as Hyde told the detective chief inspector where Teresa had last been.

Pacheco opened and then closed his mouth. He glanced between the cousins before taking off. His "Stay here" was a loud whisper on the wind.

Hyde sat on the kerb in front of the bookshop. They didn't know what to do while they waited. Their fingers shook as their mind thought of a million horrible things that could be done to Teresa.

I hate this.

The wait was interminable. Emrys arrived, then disappeared once Phineas filled him in. Hyde had just stared blankly at him.

"Phineas."

"Yes?"

"Our family is absolutely shite." Hyde could think of a few other adjectives to describe them.

"Agreed." Phineas came over to sit beside them. "I make wine. All sorts of blood and otherwise."

"Do you?"

"It's... what I love to do."

Hyde latched on to something other than their existential dread about Teresa. "The village doesn't have a wine shop... bar? Place?"

Phineas nudged them gently with his elbow when she kept listing off variations. "Hyde. Your witch person is going to be okay. Jonatan is protective over the village."

"Pacheco?"

"He ordered them to leave you alone. He even suggested I leave, but I wasn't brave enough. I didn't want to rock the metaphorical boat." Phineas stretched his legs out in front of him. He picked at a loose thread on his trousers. "You gained far more than you left when they chucked you out of the family."

Hyde barely heard him. Their attention was glued to their phone, willing it to ring. *Text me. Call me. Do something.* "I should've stayed. Why did I take off? What the dickens was I thinking?"

"Mo chridhe? What's wrong?" Bram swanned up to them. He crouched down where they sat on the kerb. "Has something happened?"

For the briefest moment, Hyde simply needed everything to stop. They felt like Teresa's motorcycle was revving inside their head. It made it impossible to think, speak, or do anything at all.

Bram whipped off his long coat, draping it around Hyde. The heavy fabric settled over them like a weighted blanket. It seemed to dull the chaos around them. "Slow breaths, Hyde. Emrys might be a foresty bastard, but he'll move mountains to protect a foundling, particularly one who matters to you."

Hunching down into the coat, Hyde breathed in deeply. The scent of all things Bram surrounded them. It helped them settle—quieted the storm raging in their brain.

They huddled in the sea of heavy fabric. The whooshing in their ears slowly ebbed. They had no idea how much time had passed while Bram and Phineas had a whispered conversation. Someone else had shown up and left as they'd been lost in their head.

Hyde's eyes narrowed when they noticed Phineas acting strangely. "Bram. Leave my cousin alone."

"If he asks nicely." Bram winked at Phineas before coming over to crouch in front of her again. "The seer—"

"Fynn," Hyde muttered, interrupting him.

"The seer was here for the briefest of moments. Teresa's okay. The foresty paramedic is with her, as are Emrys and the grumpy chief inspector." Bram shoved his long, wavy brown hair out of his face. "I imagine they'll all be here soon enough. Maybe not Pacheco. He's escorting Eunice Snodgrass to the nearest police station."

"So... she did do it?" Hyde couldn't help glancing over at Phineas, who stood off to one side as if he wanted to appear not to be listening. "Phin? You okay?"

"My mother tried to kill you. Succeeded with my father while trying to frame me." Phineas rubbed his eyes tiredly. He came over to sit beside them. "I'm not sure *okay* is the word for how confused I feel."

"I don't have any of the details." Bram returned to the question they'd asked him. "No confirmation, but I'd assume it's a safe bet Eunice was responsible."

"And Teresa?"

"I promise she's okay." Bram gave her arm a squeeze. "How about we head into the bookshop? You can make some tea for yourself."

"Or you can go over to Rosa's and get some for us." Hyde nudged Phineas with their elbow. "Take him with you."

"C'mon, bearded ginger vamp." Bram dragged Phineas to his feet. "Let's procure some tea while Hyde sorts themselves out."

16

TERESA

THERE WAS NO WINNING WHEN IT CAME TO fighting off a vampire when one was a witch. Teresa's magical prowess leaned more towards food and music than fending off a physical altercation. She tried her best to get away from Eunice without success.

Teresa kicked out at Eunice in a futile attempt to free herself. One second, cold fingers were tightening around her throat. The next, they'd been ripped away from her. Her knees went out from under her, and she dropped to the ground with a thud. *Shite.*

"Teresa?"

"I'm fine. I'm fine. Relatively speaking." Teresa couldn't get the slight tremble out of her voice. She finally managed to stand back up, swaying briefly before Emrys caught her by the arms. She appreciated him steadying her. "I'm beginning to understand why Hyde avoids their family like the plague."

Emrys gently squeezed her arms before releasing her. "Hamish is on his way. I'm sure the paramedics will give you a checkover before giving you a lift back to the village. You'll want to reassure Hyde—they were worried about you. And they'll want to make sure you're okay."

While Pacheco and Constable Antonov wrestled with a belligerent Eunice, Teresa was bundled into the ambulance. Whey Southcott, a volunteer paramedic and gargoyle, drove while Hamish checked her over. Aside from a few scratches and a rather large bruise on her back, she'd come out mostly unscathed—physically at least.

"Teresa." Hamish sat on the fold-out seat across from her. He gently rested a hand on her arm; his fingers moved to press on her wrist. "Tell me three things you can see."

"I...." Teresa hadn't even realised how far she'd slid into an anxiety attack until he'd posed his question. "I...."

"Aside from my ugly mug and old stone face up front, what do you see?" Hamish had helped her years ago learn how to better handle her anxiety; it was something he dealt with himself. She wanted to laugh at his playful teasing of Whey, who was both a gargoyle and a stonemason. "Just three things."

"I see a blood pressure cuff. I... there are some vials on a shelf. A box of those gloves Hyde hates because they feel odd." Teresa gulped in air, forcing herself to take deep breaths. She closed her eyes briefly before beginning to list what she could feel. It helped. Slowly. "I smell hospital. Why do ambulances and hospitals always have the same scent?"

"I'll assume that's a rhetorical question." Hamish finally released her wrist after checking her pulse one final time. "I have... bad news."

"What?"

"You're still a witch."

Teresa couldn't help laughing. She swatted him on the leg while falling into helpless snickers that chased away some of the shadows. "You're not funny."

"Sure I am." Hamish dug around in one of the cabinets behind him before grabbing a small jar and handing it to her. "For the scratches. You don't want to risk an infection."

"Thanks." Teresa held the jar, tapping her fingers against the lid. "Saves me a trip to the apothecary. Whey? How've you been? Haven't seen you at the taco bus in a while."

"Busy starting a new project. I'm redoing the stonework on the old cottage outside Kyle of Lochalsh. The one towards the south of the loch." Whey had a deep, gravelly voice that carried easily through the ambulance. "Project might take me through the winter into spring, depending on if the weather cooperates."

Teresa rested her head against the back of the seat. She closed her eyes briefly as a sudden wave of exhaustion hit her. "There's the adrenaline drop."

"Here. I've got just the ticket." Hamish offered her a square of chocolate. "A little bit of sugar will cure what ails you."

"Is that your professional opinion?"

"I'm always professional—except when I'm not." Hamish winked when she groaned loudly.

Whey parked up the lane from the bookshop. "Kerbside service complete. Please leave a five-star review for us."

"Are the jokes part of the service?" Teresa thanked both of them before following Hamish out of the ambulance. She had the briefest of seconds before a vampire blur shot towards her, stopping inches away. "Hyde, love. I'm okay."

"Resa." Hyde lifted their hands, hesitantly reaching out, though not quite touching her. "Were you hurt? I'm sorry I left. I shouldn't have left. Are you okay?"

"I'm okay. Promise," Teresa repeated, wanting to reassure them. There was a second before Hyde threw their arms around her. "I really am okay. A few scratches and a bruise. Nothing even close to life-threatening."

Phineas walked hesitantly towards them. "I'm sorry about my mother—"

"Not your fault." Teresa cut off his apology. She shifted so her arm was looped around Hyde, leaning into them. "I'm exhausted—and smell of field."

"Could be worse. There are worse things to smell of when you've rolled around in a pasture." Hyde had an excellent point. They glanced around, nodded at their cousin, and then began walking towards the bookshop. "How about I run you a warm bath? Plenty of time to rest and relax before the inquisition this evening."

"I'll see you later, then?" Phineas waited for them to agree before heading towards where one of the detectives waited.

"Phineas?" Hyde called after their cousin. He twisted around to face them. "Village midwinter festival is tomorrow night. Why don't you come? Start your South Myrddin journey off right."

"As long as the police don't need me for anything else, I'll be there." He waved and then turned back to Detective Baines.

Teresa thought a long bath sounded glorious. "Why don't we text the group to bring snacks? I'm not up to making anything."

"Snacks, gossip, and an interrogation scarier than Pacheco's." Hyde forced a laugh. It was easy to see they were still shaken by what had happened. "An excellent plan."

The cats immediately roused from their nap when they stepped into the bookshop. They followed them up the narrow stairs into the upstairs flat. Teresa reluctantly allowed Hyde to pull away from her.

While Hyde went into the bathroom, Teresa sat on the edge of the bed. Mortar and Pestle leapt up onto the mattress beside her. They nudged her arms, clearly wanting attention.

Teresa absently ran her fingers through their fluffy fur, one as soft as the other. She barely even noticed when Hyde returned until they rested a hand on her shoulder. "I'm okay."

"Saying it again and again doesn't mean you don't feel all weird and shaky. I would. I do—and I wasn't there." Hyde squeezed her shoulder, then went over to riffle through the wardrobe, pulling out two sets of

Yule pyjamas. One had holly and ivy all over, and the other had faerie lights that twinkled. "If we're going for a cosy night before midwinter, I have these."

"Brilliant."

"Come on." Hyde set the pyjamas to the side and caught her by the hand. "Tub should be ready. I used the herbal mix Emrys made for me after the tree fell on us. It's perfect for sore muscles—and soothing frayed nerves."

It wasn't until Teresa stepped into the bathroom that she realised how long she'd been lost in her head. The tub was filled. Candles had been lit. It was warm and welcoming, everything she needed after the turmoil of the past few hours.

"There's something decadent about having a bath earlier in the day." Teresa sank into the warm, fragrant water. She rested her head on the folded towel Hyde placed behind her. Soothing music drifted into the room from the record player. It all helped her release the lingering stress from her encounter with Eunice. "How are *you* doing, love?"

Hyde shrugged. They perched on the edge of the tub, not wanting to be in the water but clearly needing to stay close. "I don't know."

"A completely valid answer."

"My family...."

"Your family is the village," Teresa insisted when Hyde seemed lost for words. She stretched her hand out to take theirs. "We can always cancel the Skeleton Crew for the evening."

Hyde shook their head immediately. "No. It'll be good for me, us even, to be around them. A reminder of who *is* my family. Our family."

"Fair enough." Teresa knew they had a point. Anxiety and fear had a way of tricking the mind, making matters worse, not better. "I'm sorry they never saw how sodding brilliant you are."

"Their loss." Hyde gave her hand a squeeze, then stood up. "I'll let you soak while I call Wok Away— maybe they'll deliver something for lunch if they're not too busy."

"Whatever's easy. I'm too tired to decide what I want to eat." Teresa closed her eyes and took a slow, deep breath.

I'm okay. We're both okay.

What a day.

What an absolutely mad day.

17

HYDE

WITH TERESA SOAKING IN THE TUB, HYDE WAS alone for the first time in hours. They wandered down to the bookshop after texting one of the fox shifters who ran Wok Away. Evelyn Tham promised to send her brother with lunch in a few minutes.

The silence in the shop was heavy. They thought about Magnus and Eunice. Selfish, greedy vampires who'd brought out the worst in each other—'til death did they part. It was so very pointless.

What had they gained? Nothing. In fact, they had lost everything.

Moving through the shop, Hyde made certain all the armchairs were in the right place. The fireplace crackled merrily. They refused to lose their joy of the season.

Hyde lifted Mortar into their arms. Pestle had remained upstairs, keeping an eye on Teresa. The constant purring was soothing. They wandered over to the record player, inspecting their collection. "How about 'A Midwinter Crown' by Away with the Faeries?"

The winter solstice album by the popular folk band was soulful yet merry and bright. It lifted Hyde's spirits. They loved listening to it during December, so they sat by the fire in one of the armchairs and allowed their mind to float away on the music.

A light tapping on the window drew their attention. Hyde spotted Lee, Evelyn's brother. He held up a bag, pointing at it while grinning at her.

Hyde set Mortar on the counter and then went over to open the door. They paused to grab two wrapped books on the "to be delivered" shelf. "You are a god among foxes."

"You have an incredibly low bar. We brought all your favourites." Lee offered the bag to them, taking the two packages in exchange. "Books for food—a fair trade."

"Always." Hyde hugged the bag to them. The delicious scent wafted up, making them suddenly ravenous. "Thank you for bringing it by. One of those is your *Spice Compendium*. You don't want to know how difficult it was to find. The modern edition is everywhere, but the one from the eighteenth century took me longer. The other package has the new romance thriller for Evelyn. It took me an extra week to get the Mandarin translation for her."

"And that's why we always give you the extra dumplings made with blood sausage." Lee carefully tucked the books under his arm. "See you tomorrow night at the festival."

Closing the door behind him, Hyde carried the food with Mortar following on their heels. Teresa sat on the couch in the living room when they got upstairs. She was brushing through her long brown hair while wrapped in a towel.

"The food arrived." Hyde was relieved to see much of the tension gone from Teresa. The herbal bath had clearly done wonders. They watched her continue to brush her hair. "You are beautiful."

Teresa finally set the brush to one side. She caught Hyde by the wrist and drew them closer. Their brief kiss meandered into a deeper one until they finally lifted the bag of food and gently shook it. "Smells delicious."

"Not sure if you mean this or me, and I'm hoping you mean it because I'm hungry." Hyde sat beside her on the couch, deciding not to attempt to decipher the soft smile on Teresa's face. "There's your favourite fried noodles with roast pork. We've got blood pork dumplings, crispy duck pancakes, and a variety of other items. Think they gave us a sample of everything they had on the hob."

Teresa took a pair of chopsticks and snagged the container of noodles. "Thank you for taking care of me."

"Well, you are my witch person." Hyde chuckled, thinking about Phineas's words for Teresa. "I love you, Resa. I may not always get my emotions right, but I'm more sure of that than anything else in my century of life."

Teresa blinked away tears before dragging Hyde in for another kiss. "I love you too."

"Good. Dumplings." Hyde shifted back, suddenly overwhelmed by the depth of their emotions. They randomly grabbed one of the containers. "Not dumplings."

"Here. Try this one." Teresa dug through the bag and handed one to them. "How about we have a slow lunch, then putter around in the shop until it's time for the Skeleton Crew?"

Nodding their agreement, Hyde thought they both deserved a quiet, slow afternoon. It would be good to put the wildness of the past week out of their minds.

They figured it was never too late to begin enjoying the season.

"I think I might get rid of the Snodgrass grimoire."

"Oh?" Teresa sounded surprised.

"Maybe." Hyde hadn't made a concrete decision yet. "I'm thinking about it."

Puttering around the shop turned into Teresa pulling out the cardigan she'd been knitting while Hyde curled up beside her in front of the fire with a book. Mortar and Pestle lazed between them. It was just the sort of afternoon they both needed.

Santi arrived first. He immediately made his way over to his preferred seat, an old leather armchair he'd brought himself once upon a time. "Heard you had an exciting morning."

"An exciting week." Hyde took the box of treats that he handed to them. They opened it to find a selection of spiced chocolates, grabbing one before placing the box on the coffee table. "Where's Morrigan?"

"Running late. She'll be here soon enough."

The door opened again, revealing Winnie and Flossie. They waved wildly, making their way over to their chairs. Both were old-fashioned, Edwardian-styled ones, plush and wildly coloured.

"Hello, poppet." Winnie bustled over to them. Her grey hair was pinned back by a brightly jewelled pin resembling a holly branch. She flounced into her preferred armchair, setting her quilted project bag in her lap. "Flossie and I are whipping up a cauldron to cleanse the village of... villainy."

"Villainy?"

"Murders. Villainy." Winnie leaned forwards to set a tin of biscuits on the coffee table. "Always enjoyed the word. Villainy."

"The syllables are satisfying," Hyde agreed.

They rummaged through the cabinets behind the counter, hunting for a basket of bookmarks. A project they'd started in January—gifts for the exchange during the midwinter festival. They had one left to finish.

Part of the tradition was a feast and gift exchange at midnight. The presents were small and always handmade. Sometimes, villagers worked together or, alternately, made something for the entire village to enjoy as a whole.

This year, Hyde crocheted bookmarks with autumnal leaves and a dangling charm blessed by Emrys. They'd put all their love into the small gifts. It would be fun to see everyone's reactions since they'd embroidered individual names on each.

The rest of the knitting circle had worked together on a project. Partially crocheted, partially embroidered, the group had made a beautiful tapestry of a village map. It had all the shops, the loch, the lighthouse, and everything else that made South Myrddin special.

The tapestry had been a labour of love for all of them. Hyde had kept the secret for them while they worked on it at the shop on Skeleton Crew evenings. It was going to make for an extra special midwinter surprise.

"You okay, sweetie?" Santi drew Hyde out of their thoughts.

"I am." Hyde nodded. They considered for a moment before being more honest. "I will be."

And it was true. Hyde had no doubts things would work out. The danger had passed. Now, they had to allow themselves the time to process.

I will be.

Everything is going to be okay, eventually.

After everyone settled in to knit, Hyde lost themselves in the bookmark. It was the one project they had on the go that didn't involve Teresa's gift. They still had one last addition for that but planned to get it in a few days so they had time to finish embroidering the little tacos on the edge of the scarf.

With music playing in the background, Hyde enjoyed the steady hum of gossip and the snacks. The best part of the knitting group was that no one minded if they were silent. There were more than enough people to chat with.

Hyde glanced up at Teresa after a while, smiling at her. "I love our village."

"Me too."

18

TERESA

For what seemed like the first time in ages, Teresa had a regular start to her morning. She had coffee and croissants with Hyde before prepping for the day. There was extra stuff to do for the festival later; she planned to contribute tacos for the feast.

The day flew by. Teresa had only opened up the taco bus for a few hours at lunch, intent on being prepared for the festival in the evening. She met Hyde in the shop late in the evening, ready to head down to the park for the festivities.

It had been the most ordinary day either of them had in what felt like ages. Teresa hoped it was a sign of good things to come. A hint of an end to the odd string of murders around the village.

"One second." Hyde grabbed a journal off the counter.

"What are you going to do with it?" Teresa watched Hyde secure the Snodgrass grimoire in the shop lockbox. "You mentioned last night about not wanting it."

"Send it to my cousin Jade. She can have it and be the next matriarch of the family. If I'm in charge of decisions, that is my first and only one."

"Jade?"

"She's a decade or so older than me. Eldest daughter of one of my father's cousins. The family tree is... complex. The lead singer of Jaded Queen, the indie punk band." Hyde closed the safe door and stood up. "I've transcribed what I wanted to start my own grimoire. It doesn't feel right to hold the Snodgrass one. Someone else can take the responsibility. My family is here. I'll create my own history—my own story."

"So, what you're saying is the younger generation of Snodgrasses are playing pass-the-parcel with a priceless family grimoire," Teresa teased, making sure to smile so Hyde knew it was a joke. "It's a wonderful idea. You can wash your hands of them. Have you gotten the book to make your journal?"

"Not yet."

Teresa noticed the tension in Hyde and decided not to push further. Sometimes, they needed to marinate on their ideas. "You ready to go?"

"Yes." Hyde stood back up and grabbed the basket of bookmarks off the counter. "I made an extra one for Bram without the charm. He'd sense Emrys on it."

"Well, it wouldn't be a family holiday meal without a little drama." Teresa waited until they were outside to slip her hand into Hyde's. "Oh, I do love the smell at this time of year."

"Crisp air. Oranges. Rosemary. Cran—" Hyde cut themselves off from listing what they scented when they noticed Pacheco striding across the lane towards them. "I'm not giving you a gift."

Pacheco seemed bemused by the blunt statement. "Okay."

"How can we help you, DCI Pacheco?" Teresa cleared her throat, trying hard not to burst out laughing.

"I'll only take a moment. I know the night grows cold, and the festival awaits." Pacheco fell into step with them as they continued towards the park. "Eunice has been arrested for the murder of Magnus along with the attempted murder of you both. She asked for her solicitor immediately, refusing to answer any questions. The court has made an emergency injunction to put her on remand. The coven prosecution service will likely want to speak to you both about your testimony. It'll probably be sometime in January before a trial date is set."

"I... don't want anything to do with any of them." Hyde stared off towards the park, where tendrils of smoke were visible above the trees. "But I will testify if required."

"Fair enough. Enjoy the festival." Pacheco broke off from them, heading towards The Golden Puff.

Teresa hoped he didn't wreck his niece's mood for the upcoming festival. "Let's go feast."

"There's trouble." Hyde nodded towards the park entrance. Reuben Rutherford appeared to be scolding one of his pack. "I can't make out what they're saying."

"Never stick your nose in a werewolf's business. They might just bite it off." Teresa remembered her nan telling her that many times when she'd been young. "The nose, mind you, not the business."

The lamps in the village burned brighter as they always did at midwinter. Cauldrons had been brought to the park. They simmered with a mixture of fruits and herbs, all heralding good things for the coming season.

"Pretty sure Reuben doesn't eat nose." Hyde snickered. They tightened their hold on Teresa's hand, dragging her into the park. "Not my werewolf, not my circus."

"That should be our new motto to avoid police entanglement in the future. Not our circus." She laughed along with Hyde. "I suppose it's not the catchiest of phrases."

"It is concise." They peered around the park, following the path of cauldrons, torches, and strings of faerie lights. It took no time at all to arrive at the main bonfire. "Do you think Pacheco and Emrys really had some sort of romantic entanglement?"

"He admitted as much. And I mean, I could see it."

"I'd really rather not." Hyde shook their head. "It breaks my brain just imagining it. They're so different."

"Opposites do attract." Teresa could see Hyde wasn't convinced. "Maybe there's a side of Pacheco we don't see."

"There is definitely a side you don't see." Rosa slipped up beside them. She smiled brightly at the two of them when she noticed their joined hands. "I heard the tiniest sliver of gossip recently."

"Yes?" Teresa leaned in closer, as did Hyde. "Gossip you can share?"

"It turns out my *dear* old Uncle Jonatan is a heartbreaker." Rosa infused a hefty dose of sarcasm into her words. "He and Emrys were in love, supposedly. Because of the fractured relationship between druids and vampires at the time, the leader of the Pacheco coven refused to allow them to be together. And you know how he is; he follows the rules to the letter, even if it involves wrecking his romance."

Teresa knew vampires and druids had historically been at odds. Things had gotten better in the past decade or so. It was hard to imagine younger versions of Pacheco and Emrys in love. "That's sad."

A fiddle and pipe began to play from the edge of the gathering crowd, interrupting their gossiping session. Bram strummed his guitar a few times before joining in the mix. Teresa longed to add her voice.

The melody thrummed through her being. Teresa knew she'd be singing before the night was out. The magic tingled in her, demanding it.

Teresa followed Hyde further into the park and up to the ritual bonfire. Logs for Yule had been specifically brought from Fraser's farm and Ada's orchard. "Ready?

"Ready." Hyde held her hand while reaching into their pocket for a scrap of paper. "Here's to a new season."

As the villagers threw their papers into the flames, music picked up around the circle. Teresa slipped her arms around Hyde, swaying to the sound. She joined Bram in song, this time unable to stay silent. Their voices blended in with others, offering a haunting welcome to winter and a fresh start.

The festival had been a tradition in the village for centuries. Teresa had taken part every year since she'd moved to South Myrddin. None of the traditions changed, though sometimes the music did.

"Hello." Bram slipped up behind them once he'd finished singing for the moment. He handed a small bound book to Hyde. "I found a collection of poems by Nessie for you."

"Really? Poems by Ness MacDougal?" Hyde grasped it in their hands, staring down at it in awe. "Where'd you find this?

"In my pocket?" Bram teased with a roguish grin. "In my travels. It was hidden in amongst a few other items, or I'd have given it to you sooner."

"I thought I was supposed to be hunting a book on Ness for you?"

"And? I'll let you keep that one too." Bram shrugged.

"You—"

Before Hyde could respond, loud shouts interrupted them. They turned to find Emrys and Hamish decked out in robes, beginning one of their contributions to the festival—a nod to Alban Arthan, the druid winter solstice celebration. They acted out a ceremonial battle between the Holly King and the Oak King.

Their crowns balanced precariously on their heads while they fought, and their staves clashed against each other. The two always threw themselves into the mock battle. It was a long-standing part of the midwinter festival.

Emrys had a crown of holly and ivy while clad in a golden robe and holding a stave. He bowed low to the Oak King. "Behold the end of one season."

Hamish had his own crown, threaded with mistletoe. His red robes and oak staff signalled his role as Oak King. He nodded to Emrys with a broad smile. "And the beginning of another."

The villagers all clapped and cheered for the two. Teresa had no idea how accurate any of it was; her knowledge of druid rituals was limited. They all enjoyed the chaotic fun.

Emrys's staff was tossed ceremoniously onto the bonfire. He stood before the roaring flames and bowed his head. Silence fell over the park as he began weaving a tale of the first foundling. "A lonely, scrawny witch. No more than nine or ten…"

The music picked up once the story ended. Teresa joined in singing for a second time. Hyde sat beside her, sipping a cup of mulled blood wine and listening.

As the final minutes ticked by, Emrys drew the music to a close. He led everyone to the feast. Everything had already been set out in preparation.

Long wooden tables had been set up around the ritual bonfire at the centre of Raven Park. Plates of all manner of delicious fare covered them. All the village restaurants contributed to the feast—their gift to everyone.

They gathered around the tables, exchanging gifts and food by candlelight. Teresa sat beside Hyde, pressed close to them. They both waved to Phineas, who sat further down the table near Bram. It was good to see him here.

She thought about her wishes for the new year. Simple and straightforward—for the most part. Ones that had come from the heart.

Let it be a good year with joy and laughter. Good food. Adventures. Let our love flourish.

And may this be the end of our brushes with murder and mayhem.

Teresa thought the last part might be wishful thinking. She turned to kiss the side of Hyde's head. "Blessed Yule, love."

"Blessed Yule, Resa."

The End

ACKNOWLEDGMENTS

A massive thank-you to my brilliant betas and the crew in my Cozies by the Fire group who helped brainstorm some of the names in the book. To Becky, Kristin, and all the fantastic people at Tangled Tree and Hot Tree Publishing. And also to my beloved hubby, who keeps me from losing my mind while I'm stressing over word counts.

And lastly, thank you, readers, for following me on my writing journey. I hope you enjoyed *A Merry Murderous Midwinter* and are looking forward to Book Four.

ABOUT THE AUTHOR

Dahlia Donovan wrote her first romance series after a crazy dream about shifters and damsels in distress. She prefers irreverent humour and unconventional characters. An autistic and occasional hermit, her life wouldn't be complete without her husband and her massive collection of books and video games.

Don't miss out on new releases, exclusive give-aways, and much more!

JOIN DAHLIA'S NEWSLETTER:

HTTP://EEPURL.COM/Q0N0X

JOIN HER READER GROUP:

WWW.FACEBOOK.COM/GROUPS/

1108750876162947

SHE'D LOVE TO HEAR FROM YOU DIRECTLY, TOO. PLEASE FEEL FREE TO EMAIL HER AT DAHLIA@DAHLIADONOVAN.COM OR CHECK OUT HER WEBSITE HTTPS://DAHLIADONOVAN.COM/ FOR UPDATES.

facebook.com/dahliadonovan

instagram.com/dahliadonovanauthor

pinterest.com/dahliadonovan

ABOUT THE PUBLISHER

Hot Tree Publishing loves love. Publishing adult romantic fiction, HTPubs are all about diverse reads featuring heroes and heroines to swoon over. Since opening in 2015, HTPubs have published more than 300 titles across the wide and diverse range of romantic genres. If you're chasing a happily ever after in your favourite subgenre, HTPubs have you covered.

Interested in discovering more amazing reads brought to you by Hot Tree Publishing? Head over to the website for information:

WWW.HOTTREEPUBLISHING.COM

facebook.com/hottreepublishing

instagram.com/hottreepublishing

tiktok.com/@hottreepublishing